The Mail Wagon Mystery

by May Justus

Cover design by Phillip Colhouer
Cover illustration by Nada Serafimovic
Illustrations by Lucia Patton
This unabridged version has updated grammar and spelling.
First published in 1940
© 2019 Jenny Phillips
goodandbeautiful.com

To
Margaret Raymond
because I admire her as a writer,
and treasure her as a friend

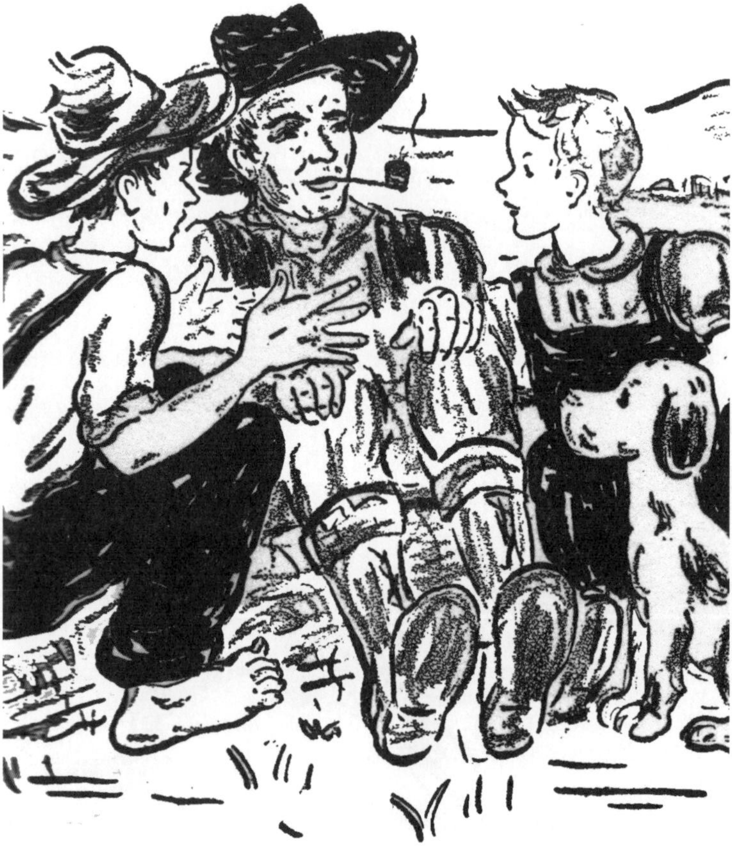

Table of Contents

1. Over the Mountain 1
2. Trouble at Far Beyant 8
3. New Kin 16
4. Out on Bail 24
5. A New Friend and a New Job 29
6. The Warning 39
7. Good News and Bad News 48
8. Something Turns Up 54
9. Dick's Story 64
10. The House on Orchard Hill 70
11. Trouble on the Trail 79
12. The Meeting at the Mine 90
13. An Unexpected Guest 102
14. The Day After 111
15. Another Runaway 126
16. Home on Orchard Hill 139

Chapter 1
Over the Mountain

In the dining room of the parsonage, the Murrays were eating supper by the flickering light from three inches of rose-colored candle. The candle was not a festive note—it was serving from necessity, since the Light and Power Company had cut off the lights the day before.

"Let's take an oil can to church next Sunday and take up a contribution," suggested Dick, who was thirteen and had a sense of humor which tempted him at times beyond the borderline of perfect propriety.

"Why, Dick!" said eighteen-year-old Harriet, who tried to speak to him severely and reprove him in a grave, sisterly way and failed to do her full duty. After all, it was Dick's fun and foolishness which had relieved the tension of these trying days. It was he who made fun of their makeshifts at housekeeping all by themselves. It was he who thought of cheerful news for Mother and who assured Father in every letter that things were all right and getting better!

A month ago Mother had become ill, so ill that it had been decided best to take her to Asheville, where she could have the best of medical care. She was still there and Father was with her. There was some improvement, very slow, but sure, according to Father's letters. However, no homecoming was in sight yet. Meanwhile the rest of the family, the Murray Six, as the neighbors called them, was having a hard time of it making ends meet. The neighbors were kind. They contributed food from their own little patches and gardens, and one who had a cow gave milk for Billy Boy. But there were so many expenses for which there must be ready money. Harriet often wondered how her mother had made such a tiny income answer the endless demands upon it. Mother had always managed; always she seemed to be able to provide for just one more need. But Mother had had much practice in the gentle art of economy, and Harriet lacked her experience. After she had totally failed at first to make the household expenses and the money come out even, she had found a little book marked BUDGET hanging on a nail in her mother's room. This contained a plan for spending which helped her out, and since then the management had gone more smoothly.

Still, there were numerous difficulties. The budget notes had no plan for such emergencies as Nancy's need for a graduation dress or shoes for John and Joan who, being twins, wore out their clothes together, as they did other things. Nancy's dress had taken the light money last month. Now the new shoes had taken it again, hence the need for eating their supper tonight by the light of an old Christmas candle.

"Any more bread?" asked John.

"Or soup?" added Joan.

"No more bread," replied Harriet, "but some very nice hot potatoes." She went to the kitchen after them. When she came back, Dick and Nancy had their heads close together over a sheet of paper.

"Oh, is it a letter from Father?" she asked.

"No, from some of our relatives," giggled Nancy, "and such a letter—*printed* with a lead pencil and such funny spelling!"

"It's a nice letter," Dick asserted. "From Uncle Matthew, addressed on the envelope to the whole family, and you stop making fun of it, Miss Fancy Nancy!" As he spoke, he snatched the letter away from Nancy's critical inspection and regarded her with scowling looks across the dining table.

"When did it come?" Harriet asked quickly to change the trend of discussion. As elder sister she often had to serve as a timely mediator between quick-tempered, belligerent Dick and teasing, provoking Nancy.

The letter had come in the late mail, and the postmaster had just stopped in with it on his way home. Harriet took it closer to the light which was burning near the candlestick socket.

"I will read it aloud," she told the group. "Some of you have not heard it."

Dick and Nancy settled down to listen with the others. The twins leaned forward, and Billy Boy stopped sucking his spoon for a minute or two.

> Dear Children:
>
> We uns have just hearn tell about the trouble in yore family and are mighty distressed about it. Can't you all come and live with us till times are better? There is room for all, and you are more than welcome. Write us when to look for you. The train stops at Slab Town. Hit's ten miles farther to Far Beyant, and I'll meet you all with the wagon.
>
> Your Uncle Matthew Murray

A moment's silence followed. Then Dick spoke: "It's a nice letter, isn't it?" He ignored Nancy and addressed himself to the rest of them.

"It's a very kind letter," said Harriet. "From Uncle Matthew, Father's brother. Why, Dick, you are named for him, don't you know—Richard Matthew Murray?"

Dick assumed a superior air. "Yes, and he's a big hunter!" he boasted. "He's the best shot in the whole country. I've heard Dad tell of shooting matches where Uncle Matt got one prize right after the other. I'd like to go to Far Beyant. Dad has always promised me."

"I want to go, too!" John announced.

"I want to go," echoed Joan.

"I want to go right now," declared Billy Boy, the youngest member of the household.

Harriet smiled over at Nancy, but Nancy was not ready to vote with the rest. There was something in her makeup which sought distinction by a subtle aloofness. It was as though Nancy drew a circle about herself, a circle invisible to the eyes but as definite as a wall of iron.

"Excuse me," she said with a slow, sweeping glance that came to rest a moment on the candle. "I'll see if I can find another candle end," and she slipped away from the table.

After Nancy was gone, the others fell to talking with much excitement and enthusiasm over Uncle Matt's invitation.

"I believe you are ready to start to Far Beyant before breakfast tomorrow morning!" Harriet declared.

"Don't *you* want to go?" Dick asked her.

"I'm as ready as any of you," she replied. "But we can't leave in a hurry. First of all, we've got to write Father, although I think Uncle Matt and he must have written each other before Uncle Matt wrote us. And while we are waiting to hear if Father has any objections to this plan of going to the Smoky Mountains, we'll be getting ready so that we can start right away."

"Hooray!" cried Dick. "That's what I say. You write the letter, Harriet. We'll all sign our names."

Nancy came back with her candle end. It was a blue one, so Harriet knew it was a souvenir from her birthday party.

When, however, Nancy continued to maintain silence about the invitation from Uncle Matt, Harriet suggested,

"Why don't you all go to bed right away and sleep on the plans we've been making? I'll see to the dishes. The moon is up and bright enough so that you won't need any other light."

Dick and Joan and John rose and pushed back their chairs noisily. Billy Boy slid down from his chair. And with an excited "Goodnight," they scampered away. Only Nancy lingered a moment looking thoughtfully at the blue bit of candle. Then she picked it up and held it out to her sister.

"Take it," she said. "You're more likely to need it than I." And she was gone.

Queer Nancy. Capricious, changeable Nancy!

As Harriet stopped to pick up a spoon, she saw a slip of paper on the floor. It was an additional page to Uncle Matt's letter that no one had noticed. She read it in the candlelight, then again, and yet again to be sure she understood it.

"I think I'll keep this to myself awhile," she thought, as she folded it carefully and tucked it into her apron pocket. "If I tried to explain to the others, I couldn't make them understand. I had better keep it for a secret."

After the others were all in bed, Harriet sat by a window, letting the night wind cool her hot face and the peace of the night steal within her. The thoughts that came were long, long thoughts. She alone, of all the children, knew the reason why her father's people were almost total strangers. Mother had told her the story one day. Mother had been a Coomer, and between the Coomer and the Murray families an old grudge had existed, dating back to a long-ago quarrel over a disputed land boundary and a lost deed—or a stolen one. A Coomer had accused a Murray of stealing his land deed for the purpose of adding to his own territory. Thus the ancient feud had started. From that former day till the present, the families had been enemies.

"Stealing Murrays" and "Lying Coomers" were the terms they used in speaking of each other, Mother had said. But Father had married Mother in spite of all this, in spite of all the protest. His whole family had been against his queer notion of getting an education. All, that is, but Granny Murray. Granny Murray, Father's mother, had stood up for him, had taken his part. And Granny had taken up with Mother, had opened her heart and home to her. But Mother hadn't been happy there with the Murrays, never seeing her own family, and Father had taken her away.

This was all that Mother had told Harriet, but the girls had understood why Father went back home alone once a year to visit his mother. Mother's own parents had both died since she and Father left the mountains, and she never seemed to want to go back.

And now came this invitation. Uncle Matt's name was signed to it, but on this other bit of paper which Harriet had found was a postscript: "Don't be afraid to come. Granny."

Chapter 2
Trouble at Far Beyant

Harriet settled back against the red plush seat with Billy Boy close beside her. She looked behind and ahead of her. Yes, there they all were, well started on their brand-new adventure. Was it barely a week ago that Uncle Matt had sent them an invitation to visit the Murray kinfolk awhile? It was hard to realize it. So many things had come to pass in the week that was behind them.

Such a mad scramble as they had all had to get themselves ready! New clothes were not necessary, but money must be raised to pay for tickets, and they must leave behind them no unpaid bills. That had been Father's one stipulation in his letter granting them permission to go. He had spared them a little extra money, but nearly all their expenses had been met by dint of hard work and ingenious planning.

Dick had sold his tennis racket, boxing gloves, and bicycle, and he mowed the yards of seven neighbors as his labor contribution. The twins picked strawberries several days and even peddled them on a commission. Nancy had at last grown enthusiastic about the trip and had found a way to earn some money by washing dishes once a day in the village hotel. They had all worked hard, but happily. Now they had several hours before them to rejoice over their victory against adverse circumstances. For a while at least, the family budget would cease to be a problem. For a while they were all as free as gypsies…

"All off for Slab Town!"

Harriet jumped to her feet at the voice that awoke her from the light sleep into which she had fallen.

The conductor paused beside her seat. "I'll help you with the baggage."

"Oh, thank you," Harriet replied. Billy Boy was still napping, but Dick and the twins were already up, their various bags and bundles all in hand, so that there would be no delay in making a rapid exit from the car as soon as it should stop.

"Anyone coming to meet you?" The conductor now had sleepy Billy Boy by the hand and was looking down on the group with fatherly concern.

"Oh, I think so, I hope so," Harriet answered. "We are expecting our Uncle Matt Murray to meet us."

The conductor made a queer sort of exclamation. "I don't think—he'll be here," he said. "I'll ask the agent to look after you, though." Harriet looked up quickly, but his face was suddenly turned the other way.

"Please tell me what you mean," she begged, but the conductor was already striding down the aisle with Billy Boy in his arms and the others following in his wake. Harriet stumbled along last, trying to steady herself as the car bumped and lurched to a standstill, and with a sudden panic surging over her.

"All out!" the conductor called, looking over his shoulder before he descended the steps.

The Murrays obeyed his order and were on the ground before he had time to assist one of them.

"See here, Miss," the conductor said, speaking in an embarrassed manner, "I guess I had better break the news—tell you why your uncle won't be here. It was in the papers yesterday morning, but I reckon you didn't see it, or you'd have known about the mail robbery between here and Far Beyant."

"No—oh, no," gasped Harriet, "but what has Uncle Matt—"

"He's the mail wagon driver," the conductor said. "He has carried the mail from Slab Town to Far Beyant ever since they got their post office out there. Nothing like this ever happened before. I know your Uncle Matt, and I don't believe he's guilty of taking the money—"

"Money?" breathed Harriet. It was getting worse and worse.

"The miners' money," explained the conductor. "You see they get it once a week, and it's sent in cash because there is no bank where they can get checks cashed. Well, when the mail got in at Far Beyant on Saturday, the special bag with the miners' money was missing, and they know it left Slab Town, so the robbery took place between here and Far Beyant. And that's all they've found out yet."

"And Uncle Matt—where is he?"

"In jail," the man answered. "It's a shame. But you had to hear about it, and I'm letting my train wait because I felt that I ought to let you know."

"Oh, yes—oh, thank you—thank you," stammered Harriet. She had never felt more helpless than in that moment, standing there by the little yellow station with few signs of civilization in sight, and the great mountains looming beyond. Just then she looked up at a slight sound. A few yards away stood a tall boy clad in blue overalls and a jumper, chewing the end of a long, green switch and digging a heel in the cinders.

"There's Matt's boy now," said the conductor. "Bob, here's some kin come to see you. This young lady is your cousin. The others are around the corner." During the few moments' conversation between Harriet and the conductor, Dick and the others had run off on a tour of investigation.

The boy called Bob came forward now, and the conductor hopped onto the steps of the car, waving a friendly hand in goodbye.

"I came to meet you uns—you," Bob said. Then a wave of crimson flooded his face, and he took off his old straw hat with one hand, as he somewhat awkwardly held out the other one.

"I am so glad to see you," Harriet said. "I—have just heard about your father—Uncle Matt. Oh, I am so sorry! I'm afraid we ought to go right back—"

"What do you mean *go back*?" It was Dick, returned from around the station house, astonishment and alarm upon his face. "What's happened?"

Harriet started to explain, then faltered. It seemed so cruel to be saying that Uncle Matt was in jail. But Bob quickly forgot his shyness and took up the explanation in his own fashion.

"The money sack was stolen, all right, but Pappy, he never took it, and nobody thinks he did but them lowdown, lyin' Coomers. We all mean to get together and find out the person who did it. Nearly everybody in Far Beyant has got up a petition to get Pappy out o' jail."

"Come on, everybody," he then called almost cheerfully. And when Nancy and Joan and John and Billy Boy hurried up, he led the way to the wagon which he had brought over the mountain. After the luggage was stored away, they settled themselves down into the wagon. The straw was a good shock absorber as they jounced over the long, bumpy road across Thunderhead Mountain. Dick sat on the front seat with Bob, while Harriet and the other children burrowed places for themselves in the straw in the back

"I came to meet you uns—you," Bob said.

part of the wagon. In hurried whispers she told Nancy about the trouble that had come upon their Uncle Matt. But Nancy said little in reply, and Harriet soon returned to her own agitated thoughts.

She felt overcome with this new problem thrust upon her. It did not seem right to push themselves upon their kin in this time of trouble. What ought she to do? Second thought told her clearly that they could not go back to the parsonage for a while at least. For the church had planned to take in a new minister who would serve them in the absence of their regular pastor. Return being impossible, she could not think of any possible course but to continue along the way they had started. Already the wagon was going on and up a rocky road that was a little better than a trail. "Goodbye," Harriet's heart kept saying to the old life, the familiar experiences, the true-and-tried path of existence. Beyond them—what?

Nancy touched her hand. "Harriet, isn't it thrilling?" There was no depression on Nancy's face.

Harriet drew her hand away. How could Nancy be light-hearted in the face of Uncle Matt's trouble, and Bob's and Granny's? "I think it's dreadful," she whispered. "What if it were our own father, Nancy, who was suspected of—stealing money?"

Nancy's face sobered. "Oh," she exclaimed, and looking off into the distance, she was quiet for a long moment. Then once more she turned to Harriet.

"It is just so hard to realize that they are our people," she explained in a moment. "They seem so—so different somehow; like people you read about in stories; kind of not real."

"Well, they *are* real," answered her sister. "And even if they do live on Thunderhead Mountain, they are our kin. Don't forget that."

Chapter 3
New Kin

    Harriet awoke next morning in a big old-fashioned four-poster with gay-colored patchwork quilts on it. By her side lay Nancy, her curly head still pillowed on her arm in deep sleep. Harriet turned softly, so as not to waken her, and surveyed the little room in which they had slept. It was the attic of a big log cabin. The sloping roof came down till she could touch it easily, and the only walls were the gable ends. In the east wall there was a little window, and through this the morning sun was streaming. Although it was midsummer, a cool breeze was blowing through the window, and the air was pleasantly fragrant with pine and the odor of wild honeysuckle.
    Harriet slipped so quietly from the bed that she made scarcely any sound. Dressing in a hurry, she found her way

down the narrow, steep stairway and came at length to a big room which served as kitchen and dining room in one. Here the family was eating breakfast. Washing her face at the washbowl on the shelf outside, she hurried to the table and greeted her relatives with a smile and a cheery, "Good morning, everybody!"

"Howdy, honey," replied a little old woman, sitting at the foot of the table. This was Granny Murray, Father's own mother, with a face as brown as a hickory nut and covered with fine, sharply etched wrinkles. But the smile on her lips was kindly and the glance of her black eyes gentle.

No one sat at the head of the table. There an empty plate was waiting and an empty chair was pushed in as if someone were expected. This, as Aunt Lissie had whispered last night, was Uncle Matt's place, and Granny would allow no one else to eat there. Bob looked at Harriet as she sat down and politely passed her hot biscuits. Aunt Lissie offered her plum preserves, and Granny handed her a dish of honey. Harriet's heart warmed to these people whom she had never seen before last night. How many times she had heard her father describe this mountain home of his childhood, tell stories of their early struggles, and praise the fine spirit of this little old woman who was his mother.

"Where're the rest of us?" Harriet asked.

"Still asleep," replied Granny. "And don't any of you 'uns wake 'em, or I'll wear you out with a hickory stick!" This threat, which sounded so formidable, was uttered with a gentle tongue and a smile that betrayed its meaning.

Harriet smiled back. "You are awfully good to us. When we learned of Uncle Matt's trouble, we—that is, I—felt perhaps we ought not to come on, for fear of adding to your worry."

A shadow passed over Granny's face. "If you hadn't come on, I'd have worried. To think o' you young 'uns all there by yourselves. We 'uns may not have so much to offer, and I guess ye're all used to a sight better, but the bunch of ye needs lookin' atter. We can do that, I reckon. I been lookin' out fer folks all o' my life. Yes, ye done right to come on, honey."

Bob had not spoken since Harriet sat down. Now he finished his breakfast, and pushing back his plate, he arose.

"I'm goin' up on the mountain to pick huckleberries today. Want to come along?"

"Oh, yes, I'd love to. May I, Granny?" It seemed natural to turn to her. Granny nodded and handed her a basket.

"Look out fer rattlesnakes," she said briefly. "And be back here by high noon. We'll make jam after dinner."

Now Dick appeared in the kitchen door, looking very sheepish at the sight of the table which told him he had missed the time for breakfast. But Granny bade Aunt Lissie bring hot bread, and she began to make a place ready for him.

"Sorry I'm late," Dick apologized.

"You won't be agin," Granny told him. "We're all late this day, but we'll be caught up with everything tomorrow. I'm always up afore daybreak myself, and the rest ain't slow to foller."

"Where are you two going?" asked Dick, eyeing the berry baskets.

When Harriet told him, he was determined to go too, declaring that he'd rather go without breakfast than miss the fun of berry picking. But Granny took him by the shoulder and marched him toward the table. "You'll set your feet under that table and eat," she commanded sternly and briefly.

Harriet smiled as Dick obeyed. How much those tones reminded her of Father when he was taking them to task for a piece of mischief! Mother was so gentle in reproof and punishment that offenses of a serious nature were naturally relegated to Father's jurisdiction. Yet he was kind too, even in his severity, kind and always understanding. One sensed the rightness of his judgment, the fairness of his decisions, and none of his children doubted his love or questioned his justice.

A little later the trio of berry pickers was winding up the mountain, the dewy grass beneath their feet, the swaying pines about them, and the blue summer sky over all. It was a pleasant morning, and the mountain had lost its forbidding aspect, the somber, threatening shadow which it had worn in the late afternoon of yesterday. Harriet looked around her and drew a deep breath of the piney air.

"Ye needn't be lookin' fer berries yet. They grow on a spur away over there." And Bob's hand pointed.

Harriet laughed and did not explain that she was looking merely for beauty. Soon they came to the berry patch. On a sunny slope of the mountain, it lay like a hidden fairy orchard, surrounded by big gray boulders and gnarled old wind-beaten trees. The huckleberries were abundant. One could gather them in great handfuls, and the picking went on merrily. Already Bob and Dick were great friends, chatting away together. Harriet let them have the conversation to themselves for it was all about dogs and hunting and wild honey and bee trees. Of a sudden, they heard a dog barking madly down in the hollow, and Bob raised his head.

"That's Blinker—yes, sir, that's Blinker. I bet he's got somethin' treed down there. Let's go down and find him."

The invitation was meant for Dick. But Harriet did not feel slighted. Contentedly she went on picking berries while the two boys dashed down the mountain to answer the dog's bark.

A few minutes after they had disappeared, she heard a little rustle in the bushes and looked up to see a flash of red in the bushes near her.

"Hello!" she said quickly, as a girl's startled face peered out from a red sunbonnet that matched her dress. Then the figure turned as if for immediate flight.

"Oh, please don't go!" Harriet called out again. "This is such a good patch of berries. You can soon fill your bucket here—mine is nearly full already."

As she spoke she went forward, and the girl did not stir as Harriet approached her. Pushing the bonnet back on her head, the newcomer regarded Harriet with a direct scrutiny that was more than a little embarrassing. In a

The Mail Wagon Mystery Page 21

She looked up to see a flash of red in the bushes.

moment, however, the girl seemed to find in Harriet's face that which satisfied her, and she smiled shyly.

"I oughtn't to stay. This patch is your finding," she said.

Harriet noticed that she spoke in the slurred drawl of her own mountain people, but there was a studied correctness in her speech, too, like that of a hard-learned lesson.

"Oh, no," Harriet told her quickly. "It was my cousin Bob who found it. It is his by right of discovery, I suppose. But there are more berries than we can gather. See, my basket is nearly full. And the boys' are ready for heaping. I'll have them piled by the time they get back. They have gone to the hollow after Blinker."

Glancing at the face near her own now, Harriet saw that the cheek beneath the bonnet's ruffle was quite crimson. The girl must be a very shy person, Harriet decided.

"Let's introduce ourselves to each other," she said cordially. "My name is Harriet Murray. We came to Far Beyant just yesterday, on our first visit to our father's people."

"I'm—glad to meet you," said the other girl, as if she were recalling a formula learned in a book and almost forgotten. "You are kinfolks of mine, too, I reckon, if you are Preacher Murray's daughter. I'm his niece, Mary Ann Coomer."

"Oh," cried Harriet, "I *am* glad. I have heard about kinfolks always—but I've never really had any, not to know or visit, or have for friends. We'll—"

From somewhere above them a call interrupted: "Ma-ry! Ma-a-ry A-a-nn!"

The girl adjusted her bonnet. "That's Mammy—my mother—calling. I'll have to go, and don't tell anyone you have seen me. Don't let on to *anybody*. Goodbye!" And she vanished into the bushes.

For long moments, Harriet stood looking in the direction in which the girl had disappeared. So that was what all the family hatred and the feud meant, here in the mountains! She and this girl couldn't be friends. Harriet pursed her lips and frowned. Uncle Matt in jail, and now this.

She turned back to her berry picking, but very few berries dropped into her pail. And when the boys came up with Blinker, quietly and soberly she followed them home.

Chapter 4
Out on Bail

The rest of the family was already at dinner by the time they got in. There was no vacant seat now at the table, for Uncle Matt had come home. Harriet was sure she would have known him anywhere—he looked so much like her father, almost enough like him to be his twin. The only difference was that Uncle Matt had a little more gray about the temples, and his skin was several shades browner because of his daily life in the outdoors.

As the three entered the room, he rose from the table, shook hands cordially with Harriet, and then with Dick and Bob. "I'm glad to meet ye," he said to his niece and nephew, and to Bob: "How are ye, son?"

Then he sat down again and went on with his dinner. There was no excitement at all, no bubbling, joyous welcome in the air for him who had just come home. But Granny's face wore a smile of deep content, and Aunt Lissie hummed a little song as she passed back and forth from table to stove, waiting on them all. As for Bob, his eyes never left his father's face, and it was plain to see that there were things he wanted to know. But he forbore questioning. After a while, however, Uncle Matt said almost casually that he was out on bail. His trial would come up later, he explained. Meanwhile, to show their faith in him, all of the Murray kin and many neighbors had made up money—a hundred dollars—for the lawyer whom he would need.

But Uncle Matt had hopes that there would be no need for the sum. "Somebody took that mine money, and it's likely somebody else knows the guilty one," he told them. "And time tells a lot of tales."

"It was somebody mighty smart," said Bob, "to figger out a way to steal that bag off a movin' wagon. But that's how it must have been done, certain sure."

"Looks like you'd have seen the thief, Uncle Matt," spoke up John.

Uncle Matt laughed. "Looks like I would," he answered, "but I guess I wasn't lookin' both ways."

The others all laughed in relief, and John blushed under his screen of freckles. "I wish I could have been along," he said to cover his embarrassment.

Dick had been eating huckleberry pie, apparently giving his complete attention to the food before him. Now he looked up eagerly and declared, "I've got an idea about how the fellow that did it managed it. It just came into my head."

Nancy looked at him with amusement. "Don't be too sure it was an idea you felt," she said. "I rapped you with this shoo-fly stick—that's what you felt."

As she spoke, Nancy waved the shoo-fly stick, which was a little green bough used to whisk the flies from the food. Dick glowered but did not retort angrily, as he certainly would have done at home.

"Don't tease, Nancy," Harriet said. "Tell us, Dick."

Nancy's lack of respect was victorious. Without another word, Dick went on eating his pie.

Later, however, he sought out Harriet as she picked peas in the garden. "I'll tell you, Harriet, if you'll promise not to tell," he told her.

Harriet promised.

"I just happened to think of that book I had last summer when I broke my leg," he said. "You know, the one that was called *The Missing Mail*—you read it aloud to me."

"The one about the bandits who held up the wagons with the mail and robbed the money bags?"

Dick nodded. "Yes. And don't you remember the chapter where they robbed the bag of gold from a wagon while it moved down Rocky Gulch? And the wagon kept right on going?"

Harriet straightened up from the row of peas and looked at her brother. "Of course I remember. But what has that got to do with Uncle Matt?"

"Maybe nothing at all," Dick replied. "But what I happened to think of was that the road where Uncle Matt went was a lot like the Rocky Gulch road, and a robber could have hooked up the money bag with a long hook just like those bandits did."

Slowly Harriet shook her head. "I don't think so, Dick. Besides, suppose somebody did do it that way; it wouldn't help Uncle Matt any unless you could find out who it was."

"But you've got to start someplace, Harriet," Dick said patiently. "I'm going to tell Bob."

"Look here, Dick," his sister said seriously, "don't you go getting Granny and Uncle Matt and Aunt Lissie stirred up with your book notions. Tell Bob if you want to, but keep it a secret. Anyway," she concluded persuasively, "a secret's lots more fun."

"All right," said Dick gruffly, "I'll have it a secret. But it might have happened that way, Harriet."

That afternoon they had a letter from Father who reported their mother's condition improved. She was still in the hospital, but it was hoped by those in charge there that she would soon be out of danger and able to be moved to some quiet place to make a complete recovery.

"Oh, I wish she could come here," Harriet said, blurting aloud the thought that came to her on the instant.

"There's room on Thunderhead," Granny said. "Even if this cabin's plumb-up full as it is, we could tuck 'em in till we could get you all your own place."

But nobody else echoed her welcome, and Harriet flushed, remembering why her mother had left the mountain. Mother, they could not forget, was one of the hated Coomers. The Murrays could take in the

Murray children—but would they take in Mother? Aunt Lissie's silence must mean that she disapproved of the plan. Granny would do it—Granny was fine, full of understanding. But the others—Uncle Matt, Aunt Lissie, the aunts and uncles she had never seen, but of whom she had heard so often, those who lived here and there in the coves and hollows of Thunderhead Mountain, the Murray clan—were they ready to take in Mother?

Just after dinner, she had overheard part of the conversation between Granny and Aunt Lissie, which helped her to understand the present status of the old feud on the mountain.

"The young 'uns would let old bygones be, if the old 'uns would forget," Granny had said.

"If this here trouble hadn't come along," Aunt Lissie had added in sorrowful tones.

As Harriet went upstairs to her room, she resolved to have a quiet talk alone with Granny as soon as possible. Surely there must be some way to bring people in the same family together!

Chapter 5
A New Friend and a New Job

The next morning, after Dick and Bob had left for Slab Town to sell the huckleberries that had been left over from the jam, a man rode up to Granny Murray's house and hitched his horse to the gate.

"Howdy, everybody!" he called to Granny and Aunt Lissie and Harriet and Nancy, who were sitting on the front porch.

"Howdy, Squire," returned Granny. "Come in and set a spell with us. What's the news in No-End Hollow?"

"No news to speak about, I reckon," the Squire replied. Then he took the chair that was offered after the guests had been introduced. "And no excitement worth talkin' about. Things have been real quiet 'round my place lately. Not much lawin' for me to do. But I got me a job this mornin'. I'm out to find a school teacher for the young 'uns. Been no school down our way since last winter, and the Board of Education can't find anybody who has got enough sense to teach the school who will live this far from civilization. Don't blame 'em much, though. The salary's mighty little and the work real hard. Still, we got to have a teacher. We want to have a summer term."

When the Squire paused, Harriet asked a question which had come like a swift-winged bird to her:

"What are the—educational requirements?"

"Got to have a certificate is all I know," was the answer. "The last school teacher at No-End was a right much of a scholar, but she didn't take to No-End ways. She went back to town in a hurry. No-End school's got to have a teacher, though. I promised I'd try to find one."

"Harriet has taught school," Nancy spoke up.

"Just as a substitute teacher," Harriet amended. "But I *would* like to try. I'm eighteen, and I've always planned to be a teacher. Perhaps the Board would let me teach the school until they find a real teacher. I should love to do that if they would be willing to try me."

"They'll agree all right—they'll be willing enough," the Squire assured her heartily. "Have you got a certificate, Sissie?"

"No, I haven't," Harriet honestly replied. "But they might not require a certificate of a substitute—they didn't in our school where I taught quite a little last winter. I am ready for college, so I think I could manage the studies of the children unless some of them are very far advanced."

The Squire laughed. "There's just twelve young 'uns, and six can't read or write their names—I reckon you'll be able to teach 'em! Could you start Monday morning?"

Eagerly Harriet assured him that she could. But just where was the school? Could she stay here at Granny's and still be on hand every day in time? It was two miles down No-End Hollow, they told her, a "right smart ways," as Granny declared, but at that no long stretch of walking. Harriet, all enthusiasm, made light of mere walking. Yes, she would go Monday morning and open school.

When the Squire was gone, Granny Murray chuckled. "I allowed as how Squire Caudil would do ye a good turn effen he could. He's under obligations," she added.

Harriet looked at the old woman questioningly, but Granny only continued her chuckling, and it was Aunt Lissie who explained.

"Last winter the moonshiners laid a plan to get rid o' the Squire," she told Harriet. "He stood fer too much law and order to suit the riffraff o' the Hollow. Well, we Murrays have been about as rough as anybody, I reckon, but we don't stand fer some things, and one is wildcat liquor. There's a good many others that feel like us, only they're afraid o' the moonshiners; and our folks don't know how to be afraid. So they sent word around to them moonshinin' rascals last winter that if anything happened to the Squire there would be a settlement about it. And nothing ever did happen, and the Squire is still plumb healthy."

When Uncle Matt came in for dinner, he was delighted with the plan. "I declare, you're all Murray," he said admiringly to Harriet. "Haven't more'n got yerself settled in Far Beyant, than you're the school teacher. I'm proud of you, girl."

Even Nancy was impressed. "Maybe I can come and help you some, Harriet," she offered.

Happier than she had been since they got off the train, Harriet beamed upon them all.

When Dick and Bob returned, she burst upon them with the news. But although they too were impressed and delighted with her good fortune, it was evident that they were full of some news of their own. They said nothing during supper, however, of what was on their mind. Not until later, when they had opportunity to beckon Harriet from the family circle and out onto the front porch, did they enlighten her.

"You know what I told you about that book," Dick began in low tones, once the three of them were alone together.

Harriet nodded.

"Well, as soon as I told Bob about it this morning, on the way over to Slab Town, he said we'd take a look at the place he'd thought of and see if it could have happened to Uncle Matt like the book said. Coming back, we got out of the wagon and experimented. It could have worked all right. Only—"

"—only it hasn't helped us any about who it was that done it," Bob finished. "So it's not much good to us, as far as I can see."

"No," Harriet agreed. "Of course it isn't. You know I told you, Dick, not to—"

"Wait a minute," Dick interrupted. And digging into his pocket, he produced a piece of paper and a stubby pencil.

"Now look—this is the road," he explained, drawing a curving line. "And here's where it passes through that steep, narrow cut in the mountain. Then here on the right is an overhanging rock. That's where Bob and I figure the robber was lying when Uncle Matt came along with the mail and the money bag in the back of the wagon. If he knew the right bag, he could have hooked it up, all right."

"And it's so rough and rocky along there that Pappy wouldn't have noticed any noise," Bob added.

Harriet squinted at the sketch. "Y—y—yes," she agreed, "I guess he could have done it, maybe. But how could anyone be quick enough?"

"It's an awful hard pull for the horses along there," Dick told her. "Uncle Matt was probably going pretty slow."

Again Harriet scrutinized the sketch. "It could have happened that way," she said slowly. "But I think Bob is right. What good does it do to have figured this much out when you don't know who did it?"

Dick frowned. "You have to start somewhere. And thinking we know how it was done gives us something to look for. For somebody who has some extra money around here, for instance. Bob thinks so too, don't you, Bob? At school, we're going to talk with all the kids. We may find out something that way."

Harriet threw back her shoulders. "You boys are going to do something besides ask questions of the children and play detective," she declared. "You're going to study, and you're going to learn."

"We will, Harriet," Bob promised. "We won't be any trouble. But if we do get on the track of a clue, you'll be glad, won't you?"

Harriet smiled. "Of course I'll be glad. And I'd do anything in the world to help Uncle Matt."

There were more pupils than Harriet had counted on the next Monday morning. For besides the round dozen the Squire had promised, there were the five who went along with her from Granny Murray's. Bob and Dick declared they were going especially to help the new teacher keep order. Nancy said she felt she should be on hand to keep Bob and Dick out of mischief. Then there were the twins who had a book apiece under their arms and were planning to review short division. As for Harriet, she was glad to have the added number for their moral support.

Just before they started off, Harriet took Dick and Bob aside. "You two will be careful, won't you," she said, "and not stir up any trouble making experiments to find out who took that money bag."

"Why, Harriet," Dick protested, "we're going as pupils. We'll recite lessons just like all the rest—and you can make us mind you."

"And thrash us if we don't behave," Bob added, smiling at her. "That's what Granny said at breakfast, remember? 'Make them two boys behave, Harriet.'"

"'And if they don't, *I'll* tend to them,'" said Dick, mimicking Uncle Matt.

"Pappy meant it, too," Bob declared. "If you doubt it, get into some meanness and see what will happen to you—at least to me."

"I'll share whatever comes along," said Dick, grinning cheerfully.

After a happy walk, they came in sight of the schoolhouse, which lay across No-End Creek, in a little clearing among the pine trees. It was built of peeled pine logs, weathered until the color of the house was a shadowy gray-brown, and fitted into its surroundings like the big boulders up and down the creek. Already a group of children was standing at the door, but when Harriet called a greeting to them, they were much too shy to speak. One or two of them did manage a smile, but the faces of the rest had little expression at all. Then Harriet caught sight of Mary Ann Coomer, leaning against a tree, apart from the rest, with a big stack of books in her arms. And with a light heart, the new teacher waved gaily and went into the small building.

Inside, the schoolhouse was dusty and festooned with cobwebs, and Harriet promptly decided that the morning would be spent in housecleaning. The children took to the plan at once. Some gathered tree branches for brooms and swept down the walls and floor. Others carried water from the creek, using their dinner pails, the lunches having been placed on a big rock table outside with a little girl left to keep guard. It wasn't work at all, they decided, but a very fine sort of play. Very soon, the timid ones forgot to be shy, and with shouts of laughter, the new teacher's first day of school was begun.

In the midst of the hilarity, Mary Ann came up to Harriet. "I went back to get berries next day, but I didn't see you," she said.

"No," Harriet replied, "I've never been there again. The boys went back once, but I couldn't go with them, and I'd have gotten lost if I'd gone alone. I'm glad you've come to school, Mary Ann."

"I'm glad, too. I had to stay home last term, on account of Mammy's being sick. But I've been studying at home. Could I do the eighth grade, do you think? I can answer all the questions in geography clear up to Africa, and in history I'm on the War between the States. I've spelled clear through the speller twice—I did that last year. But it's arithmetic that's hard. I can't understand square root."

Harriet laughed. "I had a hard time with square root myself, I remember, but if I haven't forgotten the rules, I'll do my best to help you, Mary Ann. Of course you may be in the eighth grade."

It did seem strange, she thought, to have this girl for a pupil—a girl who was quite as tall as she and who must be as old, or older. But Mary Ann's mind was on books now, and in her enthusiasm at the prospect of going to school again, she lost all trace of shyness.

Mary Ann, Harriet discovered, was the only member of her family who had come to school that morning, though she had two sisters and a brother who should be there.

It wasn't work at all, they decided, but a very fine sort of play.

"Pappy didn't much want to let me come," Mary Ann admitted, "but Mammy said if I wanted to come, she didn't have any objections now that she's well again. I'm glad I saw you the other day," she went on frankly, "because I liked you right away—even if you *are* a Murray! That's why Pappy don't want the young 'uns here and why Buck won't come. You're a Murray!"

Harriet felt her cheeks burn, but Mary Ann was so frank and sincere that she couldn't feel resentful.

Impulsively she turned to this girl who might have been her enemy but who had chosen to be her friend and put her arms around her.

"Oh, Mary Ann, let's *do* be friends! Even if I am a Murray, even if you are a Coomer. I do think grudges are wicked—and silly, too. I am glad you are my cousin. It's good to have folks who are kin to you, and if you and I are friendly, we can have a good time in spite of everything."

"I'm plumb willing," said the other simply. "And I'll take your part whatever comes up."

Chapter 6
The Warning

The splendid beginning of Harriet's teaching continued through the day. The pupils liked this new teacher of theirs who managed to keep them busy every minute. At dinnertime, they gathered around the big rock table where the lunches were spread and ate their meal together. Some of the children had found a patch of big, ripe blackberries, which had grown in the shade and were extra sweet. These they served as a delicious dessert.

During this pleasant outdoor meal, Harriet made the discovery that most of her little school was made up of her kin—Murrays or Coomers. But regardless of whatever feud existed between the families, there was no open hostility among the younger ones in school.

For this Harriet was thankful. She had already realized that it was impossible to have regular classes until the children could get more books. But at least she could form reading, writing, and spelling groups. The pupils could help one another in this way by exchanging books. The more advanced and brighter ones could help the rest. That ought to encourage a friendlier feeling and lessen the old clannishness. She would teach them new songs, new games. All this would make for a better school spirit and change the community attitude later on.

In the middle of the afternoon, Harriet surprised them by announcing: "Put up your books for a while. We are going to have some fun. Do you know *The Farmer in the Dell*? It's a singing game."

No, they had never heard of it.

Once outside, the children rushed to form a ring under Harriet's direction. Soon they were all chanting with great delight the old folk song:

> "The farmer in the dell,
> The farmer in the dell,
> Heigh-o! the derry oh,
> The farmer in the dell."

In the grand mix-up of this merry game, Murrays and Coomers swung together and danced with one another in a breathless, laughing whirl.

Before they went home, Harriet said to Mary Ann, "Try to get your brother and sisters to come. I believe they would like school this year. Tell them what a good time we all had today."

"I will do that," Mary Ann promised. "But you needn't want Buck to come. He's no hand at book learnin', and besides, he's too no-account to get an education." It was plain to be seen that Mary Ann was outspoken in her judgment and severe toward those less ambitious than herself.

Harriet smiled at her. "Let's give Buck a chance anyway," she said. "Is he older than you?"

Mary Ann nodded. "Older and like Pappy—terribly set."

That night when Harriet and her five came trooping back, they interrupted Uncle Matt in the midst of a dramatic account of some trouble in the No-End mines. And so absorbed were Granny and Aunt Lissie that even the new schoolteacher's story of her first day must wait for him to finish.

"I went over to the foreman like I said I was goin' to," Uncle Matt explained, beginning again for the benefit of the newcomers, "and he said he didn't care if there were some folks sayin' I'd stolen that mine money so that I can't get my mail job back until the case comes up in court and it's proved I didn't do it. He'd take me in there at the mine, he said. And I could start right then and there, so I did.

"But I hadn't got very far with it before I began to find out what's happenin' there. That man from foreign parts is still around, stirrin' everybody up to strike for bigger wages. He says it isn't true that the company's carryin' a heavy load and that they're payin' as good wages as they can. Some of the men believe him and some of them don't, and there's a lot of talk and it's not all pleasant, either."

"Do you believe him, Pappy?" Bob asked.

Uncle Matt shook his head.

"Before the mines were opened, real money was about as sca'ce as hen's teeth on this side o' Thunderhead Mountain," commented Granny.

"Yes, and the foreman's worked mighty hard to keep things going during these hard times," added Aunt Lissie. "Once things get to going right again, they'll do better on the pay."

"That man who calls himself Jones—he's the one from foreign parts—he has lots o' strange notions. He's the one that took to ridin' back and forth to Slab Town with me just before the mail money got taken. He always was asking me questions about what was in the bags and a lot else that was none of his business. Never did like his looks."

Just then Bob caught sight of two figures passing around the bend of the trail that climbed the mountain and crossed No-End Creek below the house. "Look, Pappy!" called Bob excitedly. "Ain't that him now?"

Uncle Matt looked in the direction of Bob's pointing finger. "Yep, that's him. Funny how he happened along right now while I was tellin' ye about him."

"Who is that with him?" asked Harriet.

Uncle Matt smiled wryly as he replied, "Why, that's some more o' yer kinfolks, honey. That's your mammy's cousin, Mary Ann Coomer's pappy."

"Tell us about your teachin', child," Granny said quickly. "Did these boys behave like I told them to?"

Not until after supper was the story finished.

"I declare, I'm that proud I'd like to start out right now and tell every livin' soul on Thunderhead Mountain the kind of grandchild I've got," Granny declared when at last no one had any more questions to ask.

"You did right smart well, child," Uncle Matt agreed. "But don't you go countin' on things being nice and quiet right along. There's too much trouble in these parts for you not to get some of it."

At his words, memory of Uncle Matt's own great trouble swept over them all. For a time, in the happiness of his new position in the mine and in Harriet's successful first teaching day, they had forgotten. Now the thought of the accusation against him seemed to leap out from the gathering darkness—to leap out and to menace them.

When, later, Harriet went up to bed, she tossed restlessly about. Poor Uncle Matt! As she finally drifted off to sleep, the sadness and tragedy of the false accusation was still her burden. Even the next morning when she awoke, she could not shake off her dread of what lay ahead.

On her way to school, Harriet realized that there was relief in a task to be done and in the fact that she had definite plans.

Her second day of school, like the first, went off well. The children liked sitting together in friendly, informal groups. The pupils who had books shared them with those who had none. The ones who learned their lessons first helped the plodders. Here and there a Murray and a Coomer were seen holding the same book.

Cooperation in everything instead of competition—that must be the spirit of her school. Harriet knew this with that intuition born in the hearts of all true teachers.

At recess, she taught the children another singing game—*Oats, Peas, Beans, and Barley Grow*. How they liked the dramatic motions they made with their feet and hands as they sang:

> "Thus the farmer sows his seed,
> Thus he stands and takes his ease,
> Stamps his foot and claps his hands,
> And turns around to view his lands."

Work and play, play and work—if these children's bodies and minds were kept busy along natural and wholesome ways, it would go far to solve the big problem.

But on the third day Harriet felt from the start a spirit of unrest in her little school. It was not anything that she could put her finger on, but it was something of which she was all too keenly aware. What was it?

That afternoon when the children started home, there was a division in the crowd. Harriet, walking along with Mary Ann, noticed that some lagged behind while others walked quite a distance ahead. She and Mary Ann kept the middle pace, though without intention.

Watching them closely, Harriet had a sudden thought. Yes, the crowd was divided on purpose. Else why were the Murray children all in front and the Coomers lagging behind? She glanced quickly at Mary Ann who had been rather silent all day and had hardly spoken on the road. Her face wore a troubled look.

"Mary Ann, what is the matter?"

At the sudden question, the girl's face flushed, and her eyes dropped. Harriet could read no answer in them.

"Is it anything I have done, Mary Ann? Please tell me!"

Mary Ann slowly shook her head but did not speak.

Harriet felt helpless, confronted as she was with this unexpected barrier which had risen so suddenly between them. Then impulsively she reached out and took her cousin's hand, clasping it tightly.

At this, Mary Ann turned her face away, and Harriet heard a muffled sound. Mary Ann was crying.

Harriet looked about in dismay. If only they were alone!

In a moment, Mary Ann swallowed hard and, turning, looked straight through her tears into Harriet's eyes.

"Harriet, I want you to give up the school—to leave this mountain right away."

Her words came with a sudden rush, as if the strength of a flood had with mighty surge and desperate strength swept away its barriers.

Harriet thrust her arm through her cousin's and drew her close. "What do you mean, Mary Ann? You've *got* to tell me the trouble. I've known all day that something was wrong, but I couldn't understand what it was or why. Is it something I've done or said in school?"

Mary Ann squared her shoulders. "No, it isn't that," she declared. "But everybody in school has been hearing things at home. There's sure to be open trouble soon. Part of it's over the miners' money that was stolen from the wagon. My father says a lot of folks think your Uncle Matt took it to spite the men who are striking for higher wages. And it does look mighty strange that the company turned around and gave your uncle a good job after he lost the

"Goodbye," said Mary Ann, turning away abruptly to run down the trail.

money for them. Pappy says that Jones says it was all a put-up job and that your Uncle Matt and the mine owners worked it out just to throw suspicion onto the men that some of them stole it."

Harriet stopped abruptly. "It is not true—it's not!" she cried. "Uncle Matt is not that kind of person. He wouldn't, he couldn't, do a thing as mean and as wicked a thing as that! Uncle Matt is a good man. And the reason he got the new job with the company is because they believe in his honesty even if appearances are against him."

"I don't know anything about it," said Mary Ann in a tone that seemed to say she did not wish to hurt Harriet, but was herself not entirely convinced.

They were now at the parting of the ways, and Harriet turned to Mary Ann with a determined effort to part in the same friendly manner as always. "Goodbye," she said, "Remember—we are friends, Mary Ann."

"Goodbye," said Mary Ann, turning away abruptly to run down the trail that soon lost itself in the trees.

Chapter 7
Good News and Bad News

When Harriet reached home, she found a letter awaiting her with good news. Father wrote to say that Mother was so much better she could leave the sanatorium before long.

"We have talked plans over," ran the letter, "and have decided on one thing: to come to Far Beyant again for a little while, if we can find a place on that side of Thunderhead Mountain. Maybe there's an empty cabin somewhere. It won't need much furnishing, for Mother stays outdoors nearly all the time. She wants to come back to the mountain, and I do, too. And we want to see our kinfolks again, including half a dozen of our nearest and dearest. Write us if there's a place around there where we can tuck ourselves in."

Harriet read it aloud. At the end her voice quivered a little; her heart was so full of the ache to have her family all together again. The cold fear that had clutched her after Mary Ann's departure loosened its icy fingers, and relief surged upward in a joyful tide of tears that could not be restrained.

The twins looked at her curiously.

"I don't see anything to cry about," John declared, with Joan echoing him. "I'm going to yell," he said. And he did, promptly joined by his twin.

"Hurrah! We're going to have Father and Mother again!"

They made such a fuss that they were sent outside to rejoice together, and Billy Boy followed to add a few whoops. Granny didn't mind. She was, she declared, might-nigh as excited as the children and felt like praising the Lord right out as if it were Big Meeting.

"It'll be a sight for sore eyes," she said. "I had plumb given up seeing my family united again this side o' the Kingdom." And Harriet was happy to see, by the expression in her eyes, that Aunt Lissie felt the same.

"We've got to find a place," reminded Dick. "We've got to find an empty cabin somewhere, or they won't come. There's got to be room for 'em."

"Is there a place?" Harriet asked.

"There's Orchard Hill Cabin," suggested Aunt Lissie. "Squire Caudil owns that, but it's had nobody in it since—" she stopped short.

"Yes, I know," Granny Murray nodded. "But that was a long time ago, and I reckon the place ain't ha'nted by anything worse than ghostly smells."

"Ghostly smells!" Nancy shuddered. "What do you mean, Granny, anyway?"

"Foolishness, mostly," chuckled Granny, her brown face crinkling into a smile. "You'd better not get me started into tellin' all I know about that old place or we won't go ahead plannin' what's to do and how it's to be done. It's the last chance, I'm thinkin'—that cabin on Orchard Hill. We'd better see Squire tomorrow; and if he'll let us have it, we'll start work right away to make it fitten to live in."

"We must find some furniture, too," murmured Harriet, thinking aloud. At the end of the month she would have her money for teaching, and then she could do things. Oh, it would be fun to get a little home ready for her dear ones.

Now Aunt Lissie spoke up with never a word about Mother's being a Coomer. "There's a bedstead up in the garret, an old four-poster. I'll make a straw tick."

Uncle Matt came in and interrupted their happy planning with a bit of bad news he had gathered that day.

"That fellow Jones," he told then, "is a prime troublemaker, I guess. He's going up and down the mountain putting crazy notions into everybody's head. He's got the whole Coomer tribe with him, and others, too, I am sorry to say. Whenever I try to reason with them, they think I am on the Company's side. And I am, in a way," he added, "but that's because I can't see but one side. We've always stood together—the Company and the Company's men. They've always paid us good wages for good work. The Company has stood by the miners in good times and bad ones, too, not like the companies I've heard tell of other places. It's been bad times of late, too—and now this fellow, Jones, an outlander from who knows where, comes in and stirs up trouble."

"The Coomers are always ready fer that, even in school," Bob muttered.

Again Harriet felt the dark wings of fear flapping ominously above her. Not in school! Let the feud be fought outside but not in school where they were all friends together! Then she thought of Mary Ann's words. Was Mary Ann's warning true? Oh, it *couldn't* be.

"If they want to fight," Bob was saying, "we'll fight 'em fair. But we'll fight, I guess."

"I'm with you!" Dick said to his cousin, and arm in arm they turned to the door.

But Granny had overheard them. Getting up from her rocker, she rapped on the floor with the knobby walking stick that she carried on the days when the rheumatism bothered her old legs.

"Come back here, you boys, and listen to me. And mind you pay me good attention. Don't you start a fire you can't put out. I've seen a good many fires started, and I've fought some, too! Be careful what you do, and be careful what you say. The Coomers may pile the wood, but it won't blaze unless somebody sticks a match to it."

"I don't mean to start anything," muttered Bob.

That was his answer to Granny, but Harriet knew that his real reply was as yet unspoken.

Dick said nothing. His steady eyes would not meet the long look she gave him, and their gaze reached out the cabin door to the shadows on Thunderhead Mountain.

"I'm with you!" Dick said to his cousin.

Aunt Lissie got up to see about preparations for supper.

"You want to look in the corner cupboard, Harriet, and find a jar of huckleberry jam? I think I'll make fresh biscuits tonight."

"Yes," Harriet answered, thankful to have something to do just then. It seemed to break the spell that had come down like a raincloud, dimming the sunshine of joy and hope and expectation in her heart. She mustn't be afraid. Clouds passed. If only this one could disappear from the mountain before Father and Mother came back to their old home.

She would get ready for them, anyway. She would see Squire Caudil tomorrow about that empty cabin on Orchard Hill. What a pretty name for a homeplace! After they all got busy with plans and preparations there, it would leave less time to think of feud fights and other troubles. And it might keep Dick out of trouble—Bob, too. Yes, she would see about that cabin next day.

Chapter 8
Something Turns Up

Neither Bob nor Dick was in sight when it was time to start to school next morning. They had eaten their breakfast quickly, then disappeared. Nobody had seen in what direction they had gone, not even the twins who rarely missed any comings or goings around them.

Harriet did not speak her fear that the two had slipped away on some foolish adventure, but remembering Bob's threat of the night before, she was deeply worried.

"Perhaps they have raced ahead to school. Let's hurry on and catch them," she said to the other children, speaking lightly against the fear.

The trail that curled down the Hollow had never seemed so long to her. At length around the last curve, they came in sight of the schoolhouse. A small group, half the usual size, had gathered in front of the door. No sight of Dick or Bob. Thrusting her worry aside, Harriet smiled at the children and said, "Good morning," cheerfully. A few replies were given her, and a few shy smiles, as she went into the schoolhouse and put up her things.

"Can we have a game?" somebody asked.

"Yes," Harriet exclaimed in relief. "We'll play until time for classes."

"Let's play Midnight!"

"Going Up to London!"

"Miley Bright!"

"The Jolly Miller!"

They shouted their favorite games, running out into the little clearing in the pine thicket where they played. It was a pleasant morning with the sunshine sending long yellow fingers through the shadowy tops of the pines, and the dew-damp air was laden with a ferny fragrance and the odor of resin. It was much too bright and beautiful a world to drag down into enmities, Harriet thought, as the children made a circle around her and chose her to be "It." The children sang gaily:

> "Go round and round the village,
> Go round and round the village,
> Go round and round the village,
> As we have done before!"

Harriet chose her partner when the time came, and then she sang the words of the old ditty over and over.

But inside her mind a different refrain repeated itself in a tuneless wail:

> "Where is Dick—where is Bob?
> I wonder what they are doing!"

As the last words of the song died away, Harriet glanced at the watch Uncle Matt had lent her—a watch as big and fat as a piece of Aunt Lissie's biscuit bread—a good reliable timekeeper which Harriet appreciated using. Grandfather Murray's watch, it had been.

"I don't need two timepieces to keep me on the go," Uncle Matt had said in presenting her with this one. "Got this other one here, trading."

Harriet smiled at the memory. Uncle Matt was so much like Father, always finding a good excuse for doing a good turn! She had never written Father a word of Uncle Matt's trouble. No need for him to know about it yet. Still, she hated to have him come back to his kin after all these years and find such news waiting for him.

Harriet sighed, and then she caught sight of Nancy's face turned toward her and Nancy's keen eyes reading hers. She nodded gaily at her sister, and then called, "That's all for this time, children. We'll go in now. Yes, you may ring the bell, Andy," she said to a small Coomer cousin who nudged her hopefully.

As the little group marched in, Nancy lingered at the end of the line.

"Don't worry, Harriet, about Bob and Dick," she whispered. "I don't know where they've gone; but from what I happened to overhear them talking about this morning, I reckon they must have gone to Slab Town on business of their own."

"Why didn't you tell me before?" Harriet asked, looking closely at her sister.

"I—I hated to let on that I listened in," Nancy stammered, "and I didn't, only for half a minute."

"Well!" It was a sigh of relief. If those two boys had gone to Slab Town, they couldn't be into any trouble with the Coomers, for the Coomers lived on the other side of Thunderhead. Even so, they shouldn't have gone away without permission from Uncle Matt or from Granny Murray. Well, this was another problem, but one that would have to wait awhile.

The morning passed—somehow. Harriet heard lessons—ABC's, spelling lessons, and arithmetic. That took her to recess. After she had dismissed the room, she turned to see Mary Ann Coomer standing on the other side of the table that served for a teacher's desk. She had been late that morning and had missed two lessons; this was Harriet's first chance to have a word with her.

But it was Mary Ann who spoke first. No howdy or shy good morning prefaced what she had to say now. It came out with a rush of pent-up feeling:

"I can't come to school tomorrow!" A flood of tears followed this thunderclap. The girl's thin shoulders were shaking.

"Sit down; sit down here, Mary Ann," said Harriet comfortingly, walking around the table and leading the girl back to her own chair.

"Now, Mary Ann, tell me all about it. What's happened—what's the matter that you are obliged to stop school?"

Mary Ann drew a long breath and wiped her eyes on the corner of her blue-checked apron. In the tense silence, Nancy's face poked in at the door.

"Coming, Harriet?" she began, and then her face sobered, and she drew the door shut behind her as she slipped away.

Nancy had a rare gift, Harriet thought: the gift of understanding a trying situation without having to have it explained to her.

"Tell me, Mary Ann," said Harriet, softly.

"I don't want to stop—I don't want to stop—but I can't persuade Pappy—and Mammy can't persuade him—to let me come on. He's off on a tear, I reckon, just because you are teaching the school—just because you're a Murray!"

"But that is a foolish reason," Harriet said, wrinkling her forehead. "I can't help being a Murray, and what in the world does he have against me? Doesn't he know I am friendly to all my Coomer kin? Am I not a Coomer just as much as I'm a Murray?" she asked.

Mary Ann wiped her eyes on her apron with a vigorous gesture, as if she were done with anything so futile as crying, and swallowed her sobs determinedly.

"I'll tell you the truth," she stated. "That's not the whole of it. Pappy is mad because he thinks your Uncle Matt is playing in with the Company and siding against the miners

"Tell me, Mary Ann," said Harriet, softly.

that want bigger wages. That's the root of the whole thing."

"He never—he isn't!" cried Harriet. "Uncle Matt never did. He wouldn't do such a thing. But even—even if he had—what have I to do with it? Does your father think that I helped steal the money? No, he couldn't. It disappeared before I ever came to the mountain. He couldn't possibly—"

"He doesn't, of course not," Mary Ann shook her head. "It is just that you're one of 'em," she nodded again. "It's just that you're a Murray."

"I can't understand that at all," Harriet told her cousin. "Why, it doesn't make sense!"

Mary Ann agreed. "No, it doesn't. And Mammy says there's no sense to a feud. Mammy doesn't hold with Pappy. She wants the old feud to die out—and I feel like Mammy. Besides, I think she's talked my brother, Buck, into feeling the same too."

As Harriet stood beside Mary Ann, it seemed to her as though a hand had lighted a candle in the corner of a dark room. Clearly and distinctly, she knew that the womenfolk on this mountain hated the feud. They wanted it to die.

The Murray and the Coomer women saw alike, felt alike. Aunt Lissie had proven as glad as Granny that Mother was coming back, now that she was acquainted with the Murray Six. It was just because she was shy that she hadn't spoken up about Mother's coming right at first. If only the women could be given the right-of-way for one time. Only one big chance would be needed if the womenfolk could have it—have it all at once and have it together. They would show their menfolk then!

Mary Ann got up and, going to her desk, began to get her books together. "I might as well go home now," she said. "If I stay here I'll keep on crying, and I don't want the others to see me do that. I'll slip out while they are playing."

She tucked her worn books under her arm and started away. Harriet followed.

"Goodbye, Mary Ann," she said at the door. It was all she could manage just then.

Mary Ann did not reply, but she turned on the trail, looked back, and waved once. Then she passed out of sight but not from her cousin's inner vision. All through the rest of the day, Harriet saw before her that pathetic figure, heard the longing words, "I don't want to stop."

When the children got home from school that afternoon, they found Bob and Dick at the woodpile, but the boys weren't sawing or cutting wood. They were sitting on a log, with Uncle Matt between them, engaged in earnest conversation.

"They're up to something, I think," Granny said. "I don't know where they've been—they didn't say when they turned up, but Uncle Matt's ahold of 'em. He'll unravel any trick they've tried, if he finds the loose end of the string."

The women set about the evening meal. The corn pone was baking and the bean pot on the crane was boiling and bubbling away when Uncle Matt and the boys came in.

The twins were ready for them. Only by strict command had they been kept away from investigations of their own into that meeting at the woodpile.

"You ran away from school today!" John accused his brother.

"And you did, too!" Joan said, pointing a finger at her Cousin Bob.

The boys grinned and looked at Uncle Matt.

"Did you get 'panked?" asked Billy Boy, who was old enough to understand one or two logical things.

Dick laughed and picked his small brother up.

"So you think we've been bad boys, do you? Bob, I reckon we might as well tell 'em what we've been up to or they'll imagine the worst."

"Reckon so," said Bob, "but we've not got much to tell 'em, so far."

"Sounds mysterious," Nancy put it. "I knew it was an adventure when I heard—" She stopped, but it was too late.

"You heard? You were snooping around!" Dick accused her. "Some folks have a mind to other people's business. Just for that, we won't tell you. You can chase along, Missy, I guess, while we tell the others what we found out today."

Nancy looked so disappointed and woebegone that Harriet put in a good word for her.

"She didn't mean to eavesdrop on your scheme, Dick. And she didn't, anyway. All that she knows is that you went to Slab Town."

"Humph—then she *doesn't* know!" crowed Dick. "Well, we didn't go to Slab Town—we found what we found, about halfway there."

"We did that," Bob nodded.

Harriet glanced at Uncle Matt. His grave face was a study.

"Beats all I ever heard," he said, speaking in a puzzled manner, as if he were dazed by what had been revealed to him.

Granny rapped the floor for attention.

"Speak up. Go on with your tale, one of you. It's enough to get a body all flustered the way you hint around and about."

And Dick went ahead with the story.

Chapter 9
Dick's Story

"We've found out the way that mailbag money disappeared," Dick told them, with a triumphant look at Harriet.

"And the money?" Harriet cried.

"No, we didn't find the money," he said, "but we're on the track of it anyway, aren't we, Bob?"

The other boy nodded. "I reckon we are—seems like it, sort of."

"I believe you're right," Uncle Matt said, "or might-nigh right anyway. Show 'em what you showed me, boys. Bring it in and pass it around."

Bob hurried from the room, and Nancy broke the tense silence that followed his departure. "What comes next? It's just like a play when you can hardly wait for another act."

"I thought it was going to be a story," complained Joan, "and I don't know when it began because nobody tells it."

"Aw, wait," John counseled her. "You're in too big a hurry."

"Don't expect too much of a story, any of you," Dick told them. "We don't know the real beginning—and we don't know the end. If this were a chapter in a book, it would come about the middle. Don't expect too much now," he cautioned them again.

Bob came back carrying a long stick thrust out before him.

"Walking stick!" cried Billy Boy, and indeed it might have been a walking stick belonging to a giant, this long, slim sapling stick, whittled to a hook at one end.

"We found this poked up a hollow tree last Saturday," Dick explained, "when Bob's dog ran some animal into its hole at the foot. He stayed there and barked till we went to find him, and we found this hooked up inside the tree. Bob said it might be a bee tree that somebody had found, and the stick was a marker to prove he'd found it first in case someone else came along."

"But it wasn't," said Dick. "Well, we realized we were almost above that pass where Uncle Matt lost the money—or I mean where he could have—and it was all such a lot like the book that we decided to hide the stick and go back later and wait for the mail wagon and try hooking up one of the mail bags. That's what the bandits did in my book, Granny.

"We didn't go to school this morning because we had to be there at the pass when Allen Thorne came along with the mail wagon. We got the stick and stood on the ledge that sticks out like a roof. When the wagon came through the pass, Bob reached away down and hooked one of his mail sacks and swung it up clear off the wagon. Allen was up in front and didn't look up or even hear us till we gave a whoop—"

"And nearly scared him to death!"

Bob laughed. "I'll always remember Allen's face. He thought mail robbers had nabbed him for certain that time. We didn't tell him why we did the hookin'. He thought it was just a joke. And we didn't say anything about what we figured the hook had been made for in the first place, either."

"Well," Dick went on, "after Allen rode on, still laughing like anything, we decided to talk it all over with Uncle Matt."

"And I said I didn't blame you a bit, Harriet, for telling the boys in the first place that it was just a foolish notion from a book and not much use to me in my trouble," interrupted Uncle Matt, turning to Harriet.

"And we didn't tell you about the hook because we wanted to see what Uncle Matt thought," Bob added.

"And I say you haven't really proved anything yet, son," said Uncle Matt, kindly, "Not really. Even though the stick probably was the way of it."

"Anyway," Dick declared then, "you said you'd like to try it out for yourself. And you went along to show us the place where you let the horses rest."

Dick turned to the rest of the family. "And we got up above with the hook and the thief could have worked his trick just like we thought. He could—we decided on that much." And again he looked at Harriet triumphantly.

"Yes, he could," Uncle Matt agreed again, speaking slowly. "He could. But where is the money now? A tale like this won't clear me in the court. It won't prove anything to the judge's notion. I wish I could think of something to do next—some place to look for the money."

No word was spoken in the room for a long minute. Then Aunt Lissie rose and lifted the bean kettle off the fire.

And Granny got up and, stretching herself, said, "I'm thinking Dick's right, howsomever. This tale ain't done. And this day ain't tomorrow. There's time for a lot o' things to turn up afore we come to the end of it all. That's what I think. And may the Lord above bless us!"

After supper Harriet sat in the narrow passageway between the two parts of the cabin, called the dogtrot, to catch the last light of the day while she wrote a letter to her parents. Careful not to say anything that would betray her worried and anxious feelings about Uncle Matt, she mentioned nothing but the plan for their visit and the day-to-day doings of the family.

"I'm going to see about a homeplace tomorrow," she said at the end. "I'll write all about it in my next letter."

After she had gone to bed, she lay awake, staring up into the darkness. It seemed a long time since the evening when they received that letter from their mountain kin. To the Murray Six, the letter had seemed a ticket to what they had thought would be such a happy adventure but which had plunged them into such difficulties—Uncle Matt's trouble and the unfriendliness which might grow so strong that the school would be broken up. Harriet sighed heavily. Couldn't something be done to solve the problems? Something that would bring back happy days here on the mountain? Something that would solve the mystery of the vanished money?

Out of the dark, a hand now reached across her pillow and rested with a comforting touch on her head. "Don't take too much worriment to bed with you, honey," whispered Granny from out of the shadows through which she had so quietly crept. "You must ease your load sometimes if you expect to carry it safely. I've toted a good many loads, times past, and some of them heavier than this, too. But there's always a way out. Morning helps in the showing of what to do. Don't take your troubles to bed."

Gratefully, Harriet took Granny's hand in her own. "Oh, Granny," she said with a catch in her voice, "I'm afraid our coming has only added to your burden. And I hate to think that."

"Then don't," replied Granny. "Besides, it's not so. The money gettin' stolen was none of your doings. The way the Murrays and the Coomers set to ain't no fault of yours, either. And what else is there? The trouble at the mine, to be sure. But that's the work of that Jones. Do you see, honey?"

Harriet pressed her hand tightly but did not speak.

"And look at what good your coming's done us, child. I'm glad—we're all glad to have the passel o' you with us. It gives Matt and Lissie something to think about besides their puzzlement over that money. And Bob has somebody to trek along with him. I don't guess he'd have gone to school at all if it hadn't been for you and Dick. Do you see, honey?

"And now your mammy and your pappy are comin', and that's good, too. Likely their gettin' here'll help all the kin. For the kin'll be so downright curious to take a look at folks who went off to live in foreign parts, they'll come troopin' up, Coomers or no. And with your mammy and your pappy with us, there'll be that many more of us together to see things through. Yes, we'll all be together, no matter what may come. And when folks stand side by side and share the carryin' of their load, it's a lot lighter."

"Yes," agreed Harriet. And magically the bothersome problems did seem lighter, much lighter. Perhaps something really could be done about them.

Quietly then, with a last firm pressure of her granddaughter's hand, Granny slipped away. A cricket chirped from a crack in the log chinking. A whippoorwill called from down the hollow. And Harriet was asleep.

Chapter 10
The House on Orchard Hill

It was Harriet who got the first glimpse of Squire Caudil's cabin. All she could see was just a patch of gray roof partially hidden by the hovering boughs of gnarled old apple trees. The orchard sprawled over the hillside and crept right up to the cabin, which seemed all the more cozy because of the encircling trees.

"Look! Is that—? Oh, it must be the place!" she cried, turning to the others coming behind her on the trail—Squire Caudil, Bob, Dick, Nancy, and the twins. Billy Boy had wailed and wept to come and had been consoled only when they promised to bring back ripe apples if they found any.

"Yep—that's the place," Squire Caudil said.

"What a lovely view!" exclaimed Nancy. "Why, it is just like a picture!"

Squire chuckled. "Yes, a right pretty view from here," he agreed. "A little closer up you might see the loose chinking and holes in the roof plenty big enough for a cat to jump through."

"We can live out under the trees till we fix up the house. Camp out. It would be fun," said Nancy, who had showed more interest in this new plan than in anything they had done since leaving their old home.

"Oh, oh! That would be like a picnic!" shouted Joan joyfully, dancing up and down.

"Picnic nothing," her twin brother told her. "You've got to help with the work, hasn't she, Dick?"

"We'll have a big job soon, all right, I guess," Dick replied.

Reaching the door of the cabin, they looked curiously inside. What they saw was not encouraging. Leaves strewed the floor. Spider webs curtained the windows which were only shuttered holes in the wall. And as the crowd trooped through the door, some small inhabitant scurried away from the leaves banked high in a far corner and made his departure.

"Maybe it's a snake," Nancy cried, backing herself out in a hurry.

"No," replied Squire, "just a mouse, I guess, or maybe a ground squirrel. Come back, Nancy, I'll take care of you."

Then he stamped on the floor. "Yes, the sleepers are sound—a good foundation, and that's something. This is the old kitchen," he told them. "When I was a boy, we did all our cooking in the fireplace there. Now let's cross the porch into the other room."

Here there was less disorder. The walls were whitewashed. In the fireplace were the remains of a fire which had evidently been burning not long before.

Nancy wrinkled up her nose and began to sniff. "It smells like ghosts," she decided.

Everybody laughed at that. "Well, I'll tell you something," Squire chuckled. "I reckon it might be the ghost of my last supper still in the air. You see," he explained, "in apple harvest time I have to be kind o' watchful, or somebody else might gather my crop and not divide with me. So I camp out here pretty regular part o' the year."

"You're the ha'nt then," Harriet told him. "Ever since the children at school heard about our plan to bring Mother and Father here, they have been warning me to look out for ghosts. They say that an old man's ghost stays here at night to guard the orchard which he planted many years ago. They say, too, that he carries a lighted, smoky lantern around among the trees to catch thieving marauders. Some say they've heard strange sounds as if the old fellow were singing to keep himself company—a doleful sort of song."

The Squire laughed. "I've heard about that ha'nt myself," he said. "Sometimes I might nigh get scared o' him from what folks tell me about him. But he doesn't steal my apples, anyway, so I bear him no ill will.

"Your Pappy and Mammy ought to feel at home here," he went on. "Many and many a time we've had a merrymaking right in this room when we were young folks together. Not much difference in our ages—mine and your Pappy's, though I guess I look a sight older to you than he does—my head got white before the right time." He smiled and pushed a wisp back from his forehead. "My wife says she's ashamed to go out with me for fear folks that don't know us well will think she's about my third wife!"

Dick and Bob had been exploring the attic room over their heads.

"I'm going to have my place up there," Dick announced as he climbed down the wall by toeing cracks in the chinking. "I'll make me a ladder stairway—the kind that's fastened with a hinge. Then I can draw it up after me when I want to mind my own business," and he looked in a meaningful way at Nancy, who, if she understood, gave no sign.

"Good place to sleep," said the Squire. "When the rain is on the roof."

Then they went out to inspect the apple orchard. A few of the trees were well laden; others had a scanty crop.

"About half a crop this year," the Squire observed. "Fellow at the county seat says I ought to spray 'em. A new-fangled notion, I guess."

"We learned how to do that in school last year," Dick told him, "and practiced on the neighbors' fruit trees. Everybody begged our teacher to bring us back and let us do it again this year. They offered to pay us for it, too."

Then they went out to inspect the apple orchard.

"Must be something to it then," the Squire answered. "Might try it out if you stay here."

They found a few ripe apples on one tree. King o' Thompsons, the Squire called them, and all sat down in the shade to rest and sample them.

Quickly the talk centered on getting the old cabin in readiness—what to do first and how much the necessary supplies would cost.

"I'll be able to buy new shingles and nails when I get pay for my first month's work," Harriet said. "There'll be a lot of expenses, so we'll buy just what we have to. We'll clean up and patch up as much as we can. And we can do a lot after school by coming across the hollow and saving time that way. Then on Saturday we'll get up early and work till dark. Oh, it's going to be fun. It really is."

"Well, I'm with you," the Squire assured her. "Been needing a caretaker for a long time. And here I've got half a dozen. Good business for me!"

They would not have to pay any rent if they stayed as much as a year, not a penny, he declared. Fixing up this old cabin until it was fit to live in would pay for their staying in it that long. And they could have all the fruit they could use, too. He would need help in picking later on, and they could lend him a hand on that as well as in marketing it. Come to think of it, there might be a bit of money for them in the marketing. It was good business for everybody.

As they walked homeward that afternoon, Harriet was thinking how right Granny had been that the dark clouds would soon lift a bit, the shadows grow lighter.

That night she wrote to her father and mother, describing the old cabin not so much in present reality as the way it would be after it had been changed by willing hands into a homeplace. As she wrote, she imagined Mother's face when Father read the letter aloud to her. Her pen raced, and before she knew it, she had filled six pages with the description of the little home of her dream.

But Harriet's dream of Orchard Hill cabin was more than a pretty picture hanging on the wall of her mind. It was definite enough and practical enough to serve as a working pattern. After she had finished the letter, she jotted down a page of notes on what had to be done to make the old cabin livable. They could use clean flour sacks to make window screens. The walls which were blackened with smoke could be whitewashed at very little cost. The bare floors would be more attractive with a few crocheted rag rugs and corn husk mats. Instead of pictures on the walls, they would hang sprays of wild berries. The place would look like a dryad's house before Harriet had finished.

Flower beds should be made in the yard too, spreading around the doorstep, bordering the flagstone walk. Here Harriet would have hollyhock, marigolds, old maids, sweet William—all old-fashioned flowers transplanted from other friendly yards. How Mother would love the fine show!

But there must be cleanliness and comfort first of all. The nice touches could come a little later on.

Squire Caudil, who had promised to keep an eye open for the needed repair materials, was as good as his word. A day or so later, after a trip to Slab Town, he rode up to report that an old house was being torn down over there and that window sashes, floorboards and planks of dressed lumber could be bought for a song.

"I've got to make another trip to town tomorrow, Harriet, and if you'd like I'll bring a passel o' that stuff along. Then it'll be on hand when we start working," he concluded.

Harriet considered this proposal. It seemed, indeed, a very fine plan, but she mustn't go into debt at the very outset of this venture.

"I had better wait to buy till I draw my teaching salary," she said frankly. "That won't be so long now—the end of next week."

"Humph!" the Squire laughed. "Then likely as not somebody will beat you to the bargain. Did you ever hear anything about the early bird and the worm?"

Harriet smiled. "Yes I have, but this bird would rather not be early than to go into debt. Father never would let us buy anything on time."

"Humph. Pretty good notion, at that, I reckon. It is a pity more folks never got it into their heads. But Harriet, we've got to work fast if we want to take advantage of this bargain. Look here, you wouldn't mind if I managed things a bit, would you? After all, it's a big help to me to get the old place fixed up again and nice folks living in it. I've been thinking. To tell you the truth, there's a botheration on my mind. Seems like I'm eating the apple myself and letting you folks nibble the core. With some folks, I wouldn't care at all—or less mighty little, for it's my nature to do a fellow before he does me! But I never planned, and I don't aim now, to drive a sharp bargain on the rent for Orchard Hill cabin. I said you could have it a year for fixing it up—but that would be a cheat. When I made that proposition, I didn't reckon that there would be so tarnal much fixing to do. Tell you what. I'll go ahead and buy the stuff myself. I'll put in the windows and repair the floor. You can do what you like later on: fix the roof, mend the fence, and prettify things a little."

Harriet felt a surge of gratitude sweeping over her, and at this proof of his friendship tears came into her eyes.

"Thank you. Oh, thank you," she murmured huskily. "I do appreciate your kindness, and I hope that by and by I'll be able really to show you my—our gratitude. We'll all do our best to prove how glad we are to have our homeplace on Orchard Hill."

Chapter 11
Trouble on the Trail

The next morning at school one of the children came in with a note for Harriet.

"Mary Ann Coomer brought it down to our house and got me to bring it," the small boy said, holding out a soiled envelope.

Harriet waited until she was alone, then nervously tore open the envelope. Drawing out the scrap of tablet paper inside, she unfolded it and read:

> I want to see you this afternoon somewhere near Cross Roads. Send the others on so you can be by yourself. I've got something I want to tell you. I'll be on the lookout for you to

come along, but if you are not by yourself, I won't come out of my hiding place.

Mary Ann

Harriet wondered what it could be that Mary Ann wanted to tell her. Was any new trouble afoot? The question stayed in her mind with dogged persistency all through the day as she tried to concentrate on her teaching. And when she tried to make herself smile, she felt as if she were pulling a string behind the solemn mask of her face.

"Are you sick? Is something the matter?" Nancy asked her more than once.

"Oh, I'm all right," Harriet answered each time, almost gruffly. "Don't imagine things, Nancy."

She let school out a little early that day, sending the rest of the family home ahead and lingering after all the pupils had taken the up-hollow trail. When they had disappeared, she started out slowly. At Cross Road Bend she stopped and waited. No Mary Ann in sight. Then upon her ear fell a faint rustle—a foot moving through dry leaves. A twig snapped nearby, and Mary Ann appeared like a wood sprite.

Harriet jumped nervously. "I thought maybe you hadn't come," she said.

"I was behind that clump of trees, hiding from the others," Mary Ann told her. "I thought you'd get here before this. And when you didn't come, I got afraid you might not remember to stop at the right place. If you hadn't come to talk, I didn't see what I could do. There's such a lot of trouble, and it's all so mixed up."

She paused for breath, then began twisting her hands in an unconsciously pitiful gesture. Harriet took the twisting hands in hers and said quietly, "Sit down here on this rock, Mary Ann. Now tell me. What is the matter?"

"Listen," Mary Ann nearly choked on the words, "Harriet, listen to me, and pay attention to what I tell you. There's trouble, bad trouble ahead. They're going to dynamite the mine tonight. Don't let your Uncle Matt go there. It's his turn for watch duty. But tell him not to go tonight!"

Harriet had expected nothing so dreadful as this.

"Oh, how terrible!" she exclaimed. "Tell me all you know, Mary Ann. Quickly."

The other's face darkened. "It's that—that Jones," she said in a whisper. "He's a bad 'un, Harriet. You can tell by his face—it looks like the Devil's in that picture, *The Temptation*. And he is a tempter, too. He comes down to our house nearly every night and talks as long and loud as any preacher man you ever heard in a meeting house. Louder, even."

"And your folks—do they listen to him? Do they believe what he says?" Harriet asked her cousin.

Mary Ann hung her head miserably. "He's about won Pappy," she said, "just like he has a lot of the other men. But Pappy's not as bad as Jones—and I hope to the good Lord he never will be. He agreed to go on strike for getting more money, but he never would agree to the other, unless that Jones got him worked up to doing it."

"You mean," said Harriet with a quick keen look, "the dynamiting of the mine?"

"Yes," Mary Ann nodded again. "I heard them talking about it, and Pappy said no. He wouldn't go that far, he said. But that Jones has gotten him to say he'll come to the big meeting at Middle Mine tonight."

"But I don't see," cried Harriet out of her increasing confusion, "I just can't see *why* they're doing this. If they do blow up the mine, what do they hope to gain by it?"

"More money—they think it will make the mine owners pay bigger wages," Mary Ann answered. "Don't you see? They mean the dynamiting for a sign, a warning of more trouble that'll happen if the mine owners won't listen to Jones and his crowd."

"But Uncle Matt says that the mine owners are hard pushed just to keep the mines open during these bad times. He says they can't afford to raise their pay, especially right now when coal sales are off."

Mary Ann did not reply. Getting to her feet and pulling her bonnet in place, she looked at her cousin with a pathetic little frown between her eyes.

"You won't give me away?" she said then. "Tell your Uncle Matt. Tell him to heed the warning, but don't let on where you got word of what's to happen tonight."

She held her breath, waiting to hear Harriet's spoken promise.

"I won't give you away, Mary Ann," promised Harriet. "And I'll always be grateful to you for doing this, no matter what happens. If I can only keep Uncle Matt away from the mine tonight! But he may feel that he ought to go in spite of everything. He may think that it is his duty—to try to save the mine, you know. There won't be time to get enough others to stand up to all that crowd."

"I don't know how many there'll be," Mary Ann went on, "but Jones is counting on getting a crowd there."

"Well, I must hurry," Harriet said, scrambling up. "Goodbye, Mary Ann. Thank you, oh, thank you for telling me! No matter what happens, no matter how all this trouble ends, you and I can be friends."

Mary Ann made no answer, and Harriet could see that her cousin was controlling her feelings with difficulty. A dry sob escaped as she turned in the pathway and disappeared the way she had come around the clump of trees.

Harriet did not linger. Taking her own fork of the trail, she made as much haste uphill as possible.

At the house, she found that Uncle Matt had already left for the mine.

"He set off extra early," Granny said, "to have a little time to stop at Squire Caudil's on the way. Some business about the cabin on Orchard Hill, I think."

"Where's Dick? And the others?"

"All gone to work on the cabin. They took them a bite before they left—called it early supper—and said they wouldn't be back till dark. I never saw such young 'uns. You'd think they was bound for a county seat show or Fourth o' July celebration. It beats all—such a hip-and-hurrah over work!"

"Oh, Granny," interrupted Harriet, "there's more trouble than ever before. I don't know what to do!"

Granny looked at her quickly, surprised at the despair in her voice. "What can have happened, child? The boys and Nancy said nothing of anything wrong at school."

"Not there. Not at school. But Mary Ann wrote me a note and when I saw her—" She broke off and buried her face in her hands.

In broken sentences of distress, Harriet sobbed out the story. "Can't we get Uncle Matt to come away from the mine, Granny?" she cried when she had finished. "Couldn't you make him if you went after him now?"

Granny shook her head. "Matt, he don't know what all this stirring up of the men has got to do with his trouble. But it's part and passel of it, some way or other. And the foreman's stood by Matt, even when some of the men talked as no Christian man should about him. Matt'll figure it's the foreman who's in trouble now, and he'll stay right there, come what may."

"Oh, Granny! It's just so dreadful, I—"

"Hush, child!" said Granny. "Hush and let me think."

For long moments, the old woman looked off into the distance. "You couldn't do anything just asking him to come away from watching the mine," at length, she repeated slowly. "Not a thing in the world. Their planting dynamite'll just make him that much more set in staying. And running all around Far Beyant and trying to get the other men that're sticking by the mine will only bring on a fight. Jones and his crowd are just laying for 'em. There must be some—way—if—only—I—can—think—"

Harriet waited with baited breath. And when a sudden gleam shot into Granny's eyes, her heart leaped in hope. Granny had thought of something!

"Listen, child," the old woman said, turning quickly to look into her granddaughter's eyes. In terse words, she went on to describe a plan so daring that Harriet could scarcely believe her ears.

"But, Granny—" she began.

But there was no time to voice her doubts as to the plan's success, in the bustle of Aunt Lissie's return from a neighbor's. At Granny's excited request, she must again recount Mary Ann's warning and revelation. And as soon as she had finished, Granny took charge, describing her plan to her daughter and adding details that grew with the telling.

"I've allus had the notion that we womenfolks could do more'n we have to stop this everlasting fighting and feuding," she declared.

At her words, Harriet smiled quickly. It was just what she had thought!

"And when you come right down to it, that's what's back of this Jones getting a headway on Thunderhead," went on Granny. "If the men hadn't been forever at each other, but had been going along together instead, a foreigner like him would have been chased out long ago. This dynamite business may be just what we've been needing to bring the menfolk to their senses. What do you say, Lissie?"

"May be no harm to try," Aunt Lissie replied.

"It'll be a miracle if it works," Granny went on. "And what I'd like right now is some time to pray over it. Miracles by rights had ought to be prayed for. But we ain't got time to stop for any praying. We've got to start right now."

As she reached for her bonnet, she added, "At that, we don't need to miss praying. We can pray as we go. I never said my prayers on a mule's back before, but I will this time. Harriet, you write a note to tell the young 'uns to stay right here when they get back. And, Lissie, you go get Dock ready."

Harriet and Aunt Lissie walked on each side of Dock, the mule, as he took Granny down No-End Trail. At each of the cabins along the way, they stopped and Granny called loudly, "Quick! Matter of life and death!" At her call, the women came running. In swift dramatic words, she told her news and announced her plan.

"Remember—it's all us womenfolk at Middle Mine at eight o'clock back in that patch of woods and not a word to the menfolk!"

Murray and Coomer women alike listened to her— listened and promised. "We'll be there," they said.

No feud had ever existed between Granny and any of them. A good neighbor, Granny had never refused to answer the call of trouble. In perplexity, too, they had sought her out, asking her advice. And Granny had not failed them. From her wise old head and her

"We've got to start right now."

"It's all us womenfolk at Middle Mine at eight o'clock."

understanding heart, they had received wisdom that had stood by them well.

Now they nodded in agreement when Granny said, "We've got to save our menfolk in spite of themselves. Menfolk around here are allus too ready for a fight. And right now too many of 'em are drunk on that Jones' lies. 'Tisn't only this dynamite. They'll go right on fighting one another till kingdom come. But they won't fight their womenfolk—that they won't. I wish I'd have thought of something like this before. Remember—the Middle Mine at eight o'clock."

But although all agreed to the rightness of Granny's words, and although all promised to be at the Middle Mine at eight o'clock, some of the promises were given so fearfully and with such hesitation that Harriet whispered anxiously as Dock started off once more, "Will they come? Will they dare to do it?"

"I wouldn't be surprised if every blessed one shows up," Aunt Lissie replied confidently. "The notion's been put in their heads, and Granny's the one who's done it. Likely, they'll remember what she said that the men'll go right on fighting till kingdom come less'n we do something about it. And she's right. We've got to get ourselves more peaceful on Thunderhead Mountain; that's what we've got to do."

Chapter 12
The Meeting at the Mine

At eight o'clock, from her place beside Granny, Harriet peered at the mouth of Middle Mine. It looked like a black patch on the gray shawl of the gathering twilight, she thought, a patch on a shawl draped across the shoulder of Thunderhead Mountain. Against the patch, a crowd of men moved back and forth like people in a shadow picture, stepping softly, speaking in whispers. Here and there lights flared—the hissing flame of a pine torch, the carbide lights of a miner's cap, the occasional flash of a match—and the face of some man was revealed. It was threatening, sinister. At the sight, Harriet's heart quailed.

Around Granny, the womenfolk pressed close in silence. All were there. Not one had failed to keep her promise. But now, standing in the darkness and looking at the menacing group of men, no longer did Granny's plan seem anything but a fanciful dream of hope. Harriet caught her breath in sudden fear.

"Matt's nowhere about," commented Granny in a low voice.

"Nor that Jones either," added Lissie, peering in the direction of the mine. "One or the other of 'em'd have been speaking right up if they was around."

"I don't mind the furriner being away," commented Granny. "Good riddance, if you ask me. And I'm not worryin' any over Matt neither. He's mindin' his business whatever he's doin.'"

Perhaps, thought Harriet wildly, Uncle Matt had heard about the dynamite plot and had started right off after Mr. Jones. Perhaps he had caught him, had met him alone somewhere, out in the darkness on the mountain, and—oh!

A woman beside her reached out and clutched her arm. "Do you reckon it'll work? Do you reckon they'll pay us any attention if we do what Granny Murray figgered will help?" she asked. A quaver in her voice betrayed her hesitation and fear.

Harriet threw back her head. "Of course it's going to work," she said confidently and found her own doubts conquered by the words.

"We won't have to wait long now," Granny told them all then. "Things are about to head up, I guess."

"Do you think they've seen us?" a woman nearby now asked.

Granny chuckled. "Of course they have. But they ain't troublin' about it any. They're thinkin' we've come to help 'em celebrate. They hain't caught on to it being a surprise party."

Suddenly Mary Ann rushed up. "They've been waiting for that Mr. Jones," she told Harriet breathlessly. "But they've decided that if he doesn't come soon, they'll go ahead and dynamite anyway."

Sure enough, from the crowd before the entrance of the mine there now came a united movement that bespoke action.

"Wonder what's happened to him," Harriet heard one man call.

"Maybe word got out and the foreman put the sheriff on his trail," answered another man loudly.

"Might be. But we don't need him. We'll show 'em—"

Granny held up her hand. "Now!" she cried. "Pass the word along."

From mouth to mouth through the half-hidden group of women the word went.

"Now!"

"Now!"

They moved forward together as a body with such a determined swiftness that the menfolk stood silent and motionless until their women stood squarely across the entrance of the mine.

"Hey, you womenfolks! You get out of here!" shouted the men then.

The women did not move.

The protest gathered force. "What do you think you're doing? This ain't any business of yours!"

Still, the women did not reply. Then the men started toward them, and the womenfolk turned and walked into the entrance of the mine where they were quickly engulfed in darkness.

This was too much!

"Sally!" a cry rang out. "If yo're there, you come right back. Hear me?" No Sally answered. No Sally appeared.

"Martha! Hear me?"

"Tilly! You get right back home!"

The night air rang with indignant commands. But until a single figure moved from the mine hole, there was no slightest sign that any of the women inside had heard a word.

When a match sputtered and a candle gleamed to life in the hand of the moving figure, "It's Granny! It's Granny Murray!" several voices in front of the crowd informed the rest.

"What you all up to, Granny?" somebody cried from the edge of the crowd.

Granny lifted the candle and shed its light on the faces nearby. And when her one hand trembled, she steadied its shaking with the other and began to speak. But her voice did not tremble.

"Listen to me, you menfolks, my kin and neighbors. I'm the oldest person here and I guess that gives me the right to my say. Listen to me and you'll understand what we womenfolks are up to. There's an evil one in our midst, and he has led you into evil. It's a wrongful thing that you plan tonight. No good will come to any of you from it. And what harms you, harms us. That's why we're here—to look after you like we've always done."

"The miners mean to have their rights," somebody shouted. "Yes! Yes!" echoed on all sides.

"That's true," agreed Granny. "That's what you should have. But dynamitin' this mine's not going to bring 'em. The mine'll be wrecked, and there won't be any work for anybody. Yore children'll starve here on Thunderhead, and we womenfolk'll have to stand beside 'em and hear 'em cry."

Granny paused, but from the darkness no answer or protest came from the men.

"We haven't any guns on us," Granny went on. "And we don't need 'em, 'cause we're goin' to stay right where we are till you all get good and ready to behave yourselves. And you'll not go dynamitin' yore womenfolk, I'm thinkin'."

Suddenly, someone on the edge of the crowd laughed. And a man's voice shouted, "Whoopee! Who said our womenfolks aren't smart?"

In relief, the others took it up. "Hooray for Granny! Hooray for Granny!"

"Just a minute," shouted Granny above the banter. "Maybe you think it's a thing to laugh over, this fightin' among yourselves, but we womenfolk don't. We're sick

"Listen to me, you menfolks, my kin and neighbors."

and tired of it. And what's more, we're not goin' to stand it anymore. You men have got to start pullin' together here on Thunderhead. Man against man, cousin against cousin—the idea! It's got to stop, I tell you. You act like a passel of young 'uns. And if I had my way, I'd lick the lot o' you!"

An uneasy laugh rippled through the crowd.

"What's more, there's things been goin' on hereabouts that no Christian man should stand for," Granny now declared. "We've got to get together. We've got to join hands on gettin' things done that need doin'. And if bigger wages here in this mine is part of it, we'll work on that, too. But to my notion, more wages're not goin' to come your way by dynamitin'. No such thing.

"Those that own this mine are different from those we've heard tell about some other places I could mention. That's why my Matt come over here and stood by 'em. They'll do better by us when they can. And if you'd stopped to use the minds God gave you, you'd have known it, too, I reckon!"

As Granny Murray talked, the temper of the crowd slowly changed. Now man after man looked at his neighbor sheepishly.

At length someone called, "Hey, Bill, can we toll 'em out, you reckon, to get our breakfast in the morning?"

"Better go and bring 'em featherbeds to make 'em comfortable," another suggested.

They were doing their best to make a joke of the womenfolks' triumph.

But Granny did not respond to their lightness. Without another word, she turned and once more vanished into the darkness.

"You done real well, Granny Murray," Aunt Lissie declared when the old woman rejoined them.

"You told 'em," added a neighbor. "Don't you think we could leave now?"

"They'll not dynamite us," Granny replied. "And they've started thinkin'. But 'twon't hurt to stay on a bit longer. How about our singin' a little somethin' now? It helps to cheer a-body up and passes time away."

"It does so," Sally Coomer, Mary Ann's mother, agreed. One time before the feud she had sat by Lissie Murray in singing school and shared the *Sacred Harp* songbook with her. That seemed long ago now. And here they were together.

"There is a happy land
Far, far away,
Where saints in glory stand
Bright, bright as day!"

Mary Ann Coomer, standing by Harriet, sang with a clear, high voice, guided by memory from one stanza to the next. Harriet found herself singing too, following Mary Ann's lead. When that song was done, they all took up another, an old-time meeting house tune which Harriet had learned from Granny. It had a sweet, sad melody, but a bright thread of hope ran through the words, stringing the stanzas together like somber beads on a gold cord.

"Where now are the Hebrew children?
Where now are the Hebrew children?
Where now are the Hebrew children?
Safe yonder in the Promised Land."

It was a lengthy song, this one, telling the happy fate of many people in both the Old and New Testaments. And when at last they had run out of Bible characters to sing about, they began on the kin and neighbors. By this time the men had joined in, and a mighty chorus sang about the fortunate state of Aunt Malviney Murray, Uncle Sol Coomer, and a number of others.

"The Circuit Rider ought to come along. We'd have a hip-and-hurrah certain sure," Aunt Lissie said to Mrs. Coomer.

"We would so," the other agreed. "We could have a big meetin', I allow. But I reckon this show is over for tonight."

"You are right," said Granny. "Our job here is done for the time anyhow, I reckon. Let's go out and see how the menfolks act."

Just then they heard a loud rumble, and the very foundations of the mountain shook.

Harriet seized Mary Ann on one side and Granny Murray on the other.

"They have blown up the mine!" she cried, and her heart was paralyzed with fear.

"Tain't real dynamite, that," said Granny. "Just the Lord's dynamite. That's thunder. We're goin' to have a storm."

Now the men began to call to the womenfolks:

"Come on, Sally."

"Get out, Susie."

"Hurry up and git a move on ye, Ellender."

"We all better get along home."

The women came out without protest, found their anxious, waiting partners, and with brief farewells took their homeward way. The threatening thunder growled nearer, and the blazing lightning split the dark sky. A number of smoky torches guided the groups that hurried away. Granny relit her candle and fixed it firmly in the homemade sconce.

"Let me carry it for you, Granny," Harriet offered.

"Better maybe," was Granny's answer. "Neither my old hands or feet are as steady as they were once."

They went down the trail with Mary Ann's family until the path divided. Mary Ann and her mother were as friendly as though there had never been a feud between the families. And although Mary Ann's father stalked on ahead in silence, his presence was no damper upon the chatter of the rest.

Harriet looked at him thoughtfully. Was he still holding his grudge against them? Then she glanced at Mary Ann's happy face. No, his silence could not mean continued hard feeling, otherwise his wife and daughter would not have dared to show their friendliness. But what was the significance of his walking on aloof?

"I hope you reach home before the storm," was Mrs. Coomer's kind farewell.

"And the same I wish for you," answered Granny, while Mary Ann and Harriet with a brief handclasp whispered:

"Goodbye."

"Good night." And then, "We will see each other soon."

The first words Granny said when they were alone on the trail revealed the worry that had been with her all through the momentous evening. "Somethin' has happened to Matt. He would have showed up if he could. That I know."

Harriet tried to reassure her. "Mr. Jones didn't show up, either."

Then she wished she had kept that thought to herself, for Granny turned to her a face that revealed deep lines of anguish in the flickering candlelight.

"The Good Lord grant no harm has come to my son," she said as if in prayer.

As they drew near home, Aunt Lissie broke the silence to wonder if the children were asleep.

"We might as well slip to bed and not wake 'em up tonight," she said. "If we do, they'll have to hear the whole story, and then none of us will get any rest till nigh the break o' day."

"In the note, I told them we'd be in late and not to wait up for us," Harriet said. "I guess they were all tired enough to go to sleep right away."

They reached the front gate just ahead of the rain and entered the dogtrot shelter as the first downpour descended above their heads.

"The Lord be praised for shelter!" Granny cried.

Someone stirred inside from a bed in a far corner.

"Is that you, Granny? Harriet?" It was Nancy who spoke sleepily out of the dark.

"Yes, yes, we are here, safe and sound," Harriet told her. "Are all of you in bed? Are you all right?" she questioned.

"Billy Boy and the twins and I are here. Bob and Dick followed Uncle Matt, I think. They left as soon as they read the note, and they wouldn't tell me what they were up to or where they were going."

"Oh, oh," Aunt Lissie began to wail. "What in the world has happened? What can we do? What can we do?"

"You can stop wringin' your hands and carryin' on like that," said Granny, speaking to her as sternly as if she were an upset young girl. "We've got to wait till this storm dies down and the Lord sends daylight again before we can see to do anything. And while we're waitin', we might as well lie down and get a little rest."

Then Aunt Lissie went to the fireplace and kindled a chip fire between the andirons on the hearth. The cheerful glow that soon spread through the room seemed to warm their hearts as well as their hands. Outside the storm was hurling long javelins of rain against the roof. The wind put its shoulder to the door like a giant bent on coming inside to wreak destruction upon them. But the little hearth fire flickered bravely, defying the enemy and sending up its red banner of hope before the weary watchers.

Suddenly, during a lull in the wind, and between the gusts of rain, a cry was heard beyond the door:

"Open. Open. Open!"

Chapter 13
An Unexpected Guest

The four of them scrambled toward the door, stumbling in their hurry over chairs and bumping against one another on the way. It was Harriet's hand which lifted the latch. The wild wind swung the door inward with a violence that nearly stunned her. She pushed her hair back and peered out, the others crowding closely behind her, looking over her shoulder and crying one question: "Who is it?"

A strange sight met their eyes: a crumpled figure on a stretcher made from a man's overcoat with poles pushed through the arms and lashed to the tails. The burden bearers were Uncle Matt, Dick, Bob, and Buck Coomer. The man on the stretcher they could not recognize for the side of his face was concealed by a hand spread awkwardly, the fingers outstretched stiffly, reminding Harriet of spider legs.

"Jones," Uncle Matt spoke briefly. "Nowhere else to take him."

In silence, they brought their load inside the room and laid it down before the fire. The figure stirred, and a groan came from the mouth that seemed to open involuntarily.

"Maybe he's dyin'," Aunt Lissie whispered breathlessly.

The dark face turned from the fire then, and black eyes snapped open.

"What have you fools done with me? I'm hurt. Get me a doctor."

The little circle shrank away from the menace in the voice that struck like a blow. All but Granny. She took a step nearer and poked up the fire.

"Throw on a pine knot. I reckon, Mr. Jones, you'll have to let me doctor you as best I can. What seems to ail you mostly?"

"My back, my arms, my legs—" he groaned. "Oh. Ouch! Every bone in my body is broken."

"Not so bad as all that," Uncle Matt said. "He had a bad fall, certain, and sprained a muscle or two somewhere, busted an ankle, maybe, but I looked him over before we set out, and there's nothin' worse the matter with him."

"Humph. We'll see. *I'll* see, anyway," Granny said. "Matt, you and Lissie stay here and help me. You—all the rest o' you young ones, go and make another fire in the big room. Harriet and Nancy, get dry clothes for the boys to put on.

As soon as I see to this man person, I'll brew a big kettle o' boneset tea to dose up everybody."

As the boys went into the big room, they saw that Buck Coomer had slipped away. "Too bashful to stay," said Bob.

When a fire had been kindled in the big room, piled high in spendthrift fashion till the hot flames roared and licked red tongues high up the throat of the chimney, the boys got into dry clothes behind a screen in one corner made by sheets stretched over chairs. While they dressed, their tongues were busy for they were as eager to tell their tale as the girls were anxious to hear it.

"Buck Coomer, he warned us about the meetin' at the mine," Bob told them. "Seems like he did it on account of Mary Ann bein' so worried over it. He waylaid us on our way home from the cabin and took us off by ourselves to tell us what Jones' gang meant to do. He was scared to death that his pappy would find out he had cheeped, but we promised to keep his secret, so he went along home and—" Bob paused, and everybody cried, "Go on!" But Bob was breathless so Dick took up the tale.

"We meant to tell Granny and ask her what to do. But you'd gone and when we read your note, we started off after Uncle Matt to warn him. Well, up on the trail where it bends around the shoulder of the mountain we caught sight of Uncle Matt down below. He was acting sort of funny, slipping along as if he were tracking something. And he was!"

"Mr. Jones!" Nancy guessed. "Go on, Dick, go on!"

Dick frowned at his sister's interruption. "Yes, it was Jones," he admitted. "We saw him running like forty around another loop in the trail.

"Well, Bob and I decided to head him off, and we thought the best way to do it was to backtrack ourselves for a quarter of a mile and surprise him on the bend in the trail where it crosses the creek. There's a foot-log there. It was getting late by this time and real dark in the woods. But we hurried as fast as we could."

"Weren't you afraid he might—might—shoot you?" Nancy demanded, her eyes glowing.

"Of course we thought of that," said Dick, "but we had to take a chance, and we could tell he was pulling away from Uncle Matt. Besides, even if Uncle Matt had caught up with him, Uncle would've needed us. Jones is a lot bigger man than Uncle Matt, and we knew Uncle would have had a hard time managing him alone."

He paused again, glancing around to make sure the girls were following his story. Satisfied, he rushed on to the climax.

"Well, we got to the foot-log just as he started to dash across. When we yelled, he looked around and that made him slip off the log and tumble into the creek. There are a lot of big boulders there, and he caught his foot under one of them and cracked his head against another when he fell. He was knocked unconscious, and his leg got twisted, too."

"What did you do then?" asked Nancy. "Bring him to?"

Dick gave his sister a disgusted look. "We fished him out, of course. That is, we managed it after Uncle Matt came up to give us a hand. Saved him from drowning, all right."

Breathlessly his audience waited for the rest of the story.

"Then we made a fire to warm us by," Dick went on with vast satisfaction in their absorbed attention. "When Jones opened his eyes and tried to get up, his leg buckled under him. So we fixed a stretcher out of one of our coats. But by that time, the storm was coming down on us. It wasn't any easy job, I can tell you, carrying him along that trail. I don't know what we would have done if Buck Coomer hadn't happened along to give us a hand. Then we got home and that's all."

"I'm thankful it came out all right," said Harriet, "and that he didn't attack you and Uncle Matt. It's lucky Uncle Matt chased him, too, because otherwise he would have gotten back to the mine and then perhaps Granny's plan wouldn't have worked out so well there."

"What happened at the mine?" asked Bob.

Harriet told her story briefly, cutting it short when Granny came in bearing a black kettle from which arose a steam, heavy with a pungent, bitter odor.

"One drink around for everybody and a good one, too," said the old woman, holding out a big dipper nearly full of the potent brew. "Boneset and a dash of pennyr'yal to keep you all from ketchin' cold."

Harriet took the dipper and swallowed the first dose to set a good example to the others, and especially to please Granny who, with the best of intentions, dosed the household on the least excuse. The boys fled before her, but the little old woman pursued them with determination,

Mr. Jones was now sleeping on a pallet bed.

cornering them and making them take a good measure of the bitter dose.

"Now off to bed with you all," she commanded. "Did you know it was after midnight?"

"What about—our guest?" Harriet lingered to make inquiry of her.

"Well enough," was the answer. "He's sound except for a sprained ankle and some bad bruises. I've got three different kinds o' poultices on him, and they'll draw most o' the ailments out. What do you look like that for, honey?"

Harriet smiled tremulously. "I was just wishing, Granny, that you knew how to make a poultice that could draw out the wickedness in him."

Granny gave a crooked little grin.

Harriet returned with her to the room where Mr. Jones was now sleeping on a pallet bed before the fire that had died to a bed of glowing embers. In the shadowed light, the lines of his face seemed sinister, full of threat. Harriet turned away with a slight shudder.

Granny laid her hand upon her granddaughter's shoulder. "'If thine enemy hunger, feed him,'" she quoted, "'if he thirst, give him to drink.' That's out of the Good Book, honey, and I reckon that means give a bed to your enemy when he's in bodily pain. Leastways, that's how I understand it."

Harriet put her arms around Granny's neck. "You are so good, Granny. Good night." She turned away quickly and started up to bed. On the way, she ran into Dick.

"Harriet!" he whispered.

The Mail Wagon Mystery

"Why, Dick, what are you up for? I thought Granny sent you off to bed a long time ago!"

"Harriet," Dick's tone was excited, though muted warily, "do you suppose he could be the one who took the money?" His voice died down to a ghost of a whisper. "Maybe he had the money with him and was running away with it. Maybe he stole the miners' money. If we can prove it, Uncle Matt will be cleared of the charge against him. Where's that coat?"

"Don't be silly, Dick," Harriet began, "you've just got that book on your—"

A sudden creak of a loose board beyond in the darkness of the kitchen interrupted. Harriet caught her breath in fear. The cabin seemed so different with Mr. Jones there. But it wasn't a step, evidently.

"He was just rolling over, I guess," Dick whispered in a moment. "Honestly he could have done it, Harriet. He's the meanest man around here."

"Come out into the dogtrot," Harriet told him then. "There's something I want to say to you."

Out in the dogtrot, Harriet put her mouth close to Dick's ear. "Listen, Dick," she said firmly, "don't you go talking about these ideas of yours that don't lead anywhere. Granny's going to look after Mr. Jones because he's hurt, and it doesn't matter to her what he's like, otherwise. If you get the children started, they'll upset him and he'll be that much harder to take care of."

Beside them, hanging on some nails, were the wet things Granny had taken from them all.

"Look, Harriet," was Dick's sole reply. "Here's his long coat. I'm going to search it."

Eagerly he thrust his hands into the soggy pockets, the ones inside as well as those outside, but with no reward for his pains.

"Every single one empty," he muttered disgustedly.

"What did I tell you—" Harriet began. But Dick was gone.

So weary that she had lost all feeling except a half-numb longing to drop into bed, Harriet climbed the stairs. What Granny had done was fine. School, too, would be a happier place now. Remembering the friendliness on the trail, as they had come home, Harriet felt sure that the Coomers and Murrays would now forget their feud, or at least enough of it to make things a little better. "But what of Uncle Matt?" she thought, as she made ready for bed.

Chapter 14
The Day After

When Harriet awoke next morning, the sun was streaming through the window, and a breath of honeysuckle scented the air. Nowhere was there a hint of the storm to remind her of the night before. At the sound of a voice in the kitchen, she leaped out of bed and, dressing hurriedly, ran out to see what was happening.

Breakfast had been eaten, she could see with one glance at the table, and Nancy was washing things up. Nobody else was in sight.

"It's a good thing it's Saturday," said Nancy by way of greeting. "Do you know what time of day it is? Nearly ten o'clock!"

"And I don't feel half awake yet. But I am more than half hungry! Where is all the family?"

"Here and there," was Nancy's reply. "Granny's out in the garden. Aunt Lissie has gone to the store. The others hurried away right after breakfast to work on the cabin. Uncle Matt's at the barn, I think. Mr. Jones is out in the dogtrot."

Glancing toward the door, Harriet smiled and spoke with loud cheerfulness. "Yes, it's a beautiful morning." Then dropping her voice she asked, "What is he doing?"

"I think he's plotting something against us," Nancy whispered ominously.

"Don't be silly, Nancy," Harriet whispered back. "What is there to be afraid of?"

"Just the way he looks makes me sure he's up to no good," declared Nancy. "It's as though he's figuring something out in his mind, I mean."

A sudden shadow fell across the square of sun that lay like a rug in the kitchen door, which opened into the dogtrot.

Nancy nudged Harriet. "Those beans in the pot will burn if I don't pour some water on them right now," she said clearly.

Harriet got up. "I think I'd like some honey on this piece of bread."

With eyes upon the door, they chattered on. There was no sound in the dogtrot save the rustle of the honeysuckle vines in the wind. Yet the sense of suspense remained, and the girls were relieved when they heard Granny singing as she came in from the yard. If her stalwart old heart held any foreboding or fear that pleasant morning, no one could have told it. She sang a snatch of the tune that always came from her lips when her soul was full of the spirit of real thanksgiving:

> "The Lord's our Rock, in Him we hide
> A shelter in the time of storm!"

Her feet tarried at the front step.

"Now, Mr. Jones," she scolded, "you've got that leg out o' kilter again. Can't I turn my back on you for the time it takes to draw a good breath but you get the poultice twisted away from the place where it ought to be? But I never did see a man person who could behave when he had somethin' the matter with him. The only way to keep 'em quiet would be to hit 'em in the head, and addle their brains a mite, I guess. Menfolks are worrisome creatures."

Dumping down her basket of vegetables, she pulled up a chair and bent over the dark man who now lay sprawled on the floor where a quilt had been spread for him. Under his head was his folded coat.

Harriet and Nancy watched her from the kitchen door. Granny worked as tenderly with this stranger as if he were her own kin or a neighbor. The man said nothing. His head turned, he kept his eyes on the trail that led down the mountain.

Uncle Matt now came in at the back door with a piece of broken harness. "You girls wouldn't know where I could find a piece of good stout thread, would you? I've used up all the shoe thread I had, and this job's not finished.

Want to hurry up too, for I've got to go to Slab Town in the afternoon. Going to haul some window frames for the old cabin. Thought I'd better fix this harness. If the horses ran away, there would be smithereens o' glass all up and down this mountain. Where's your granny? She'll know about the thread."

Harriet nodded her head. "Out there," in a significant tone. Just then Granny entered the kitchen, and while she was hunting for the needed thread, the girls proceeded to tidy up the room which had been long neglected.

Granny found the harness thread for Uncle Matt and sent him on about his business while she and the girls busied themselves with preparations for the noonday meal. Granny's spirits, Harriet could not help seeing, were noticeably uplifted. There was no mistaking that.

"You seem none the worse for last night's adventure," Harriet told her as she sat opposite shelling peas to go into the pot.

Granny lifted her wrinkled old face, and her mouth twitched at the corners.

"The Lord delivered the enemy into our hands," she said softly, "and I am thankful for His mercies. Last night's trouble is ended, and the worst that could have taken place never came to pass." Then dropping her voice, she added, "Seems that it wasn't meant to be at all. What with Matt comin' along to see the furriner just when he did and callin' to him, and him startin' off like a rabbit and Matt gettin' his suspicions up and startin' after him and him beginnin' to run, that way."

"But why was he there on the trail, Granny?" Harriet asked in a low voice.

"He got plumb mixed up, that's why," Granny replied. "He was tryin' to beat Matt to the mine, but he took the wrong trail. And Matt got to hollerin' and he thought Matt knowed what he was up to—about the dynamitin', I mean—and he took to his heels. He's a coward or he'd have known Matt couldn't beat him up alone. Leastways, that's how I figure it out from what Matt told me this morning. I'm thankful it turned out the way it did. Things might not have worked out the way they did at the mine if the furriner'd been there."

"It was due to you that things did work out, Granny," Harriet said quickly. "You made us that speech. I'll never forget it, and nobody else will that heard it."

"Oh," Nancy cried, "I wish that I could have been there. I wasn't with you at the mine, and I wasn't with the boys when they—"

"Hush!" cried Harriet, nodding her head toward the open door.

Nancy left her wail unfinished, but her disappointment could be read in the expression on her face.

"Never mind," consoled her sister, "you may have missed a lot of excitement, but you escaped a lot of worry and trouble, too. For a while we didn't know just what was going to happen. I thought of the rest of you at home and was glad that you were safe."

Nancy sniffed slightly. "And we weren't so safe after all—just Billy Boy, the twins and I," she reminded Harriet.

Her voice held so self-pitying a note that Harriet reached over and gave her a comforting pat.

"Never mind, Nancy," she said. "No telling what may turn up yet."

Nancy looked a bit more hopeful.

"There's always something turning up," she admitted. "I don't think I ever read a story half as interesting as the life we have lived since we came to Thunderhead. I wonder what will happen next."

Just then Granny made a sudden movement and spilled a mess of pea hulls from her apron. As Harriet and Nancy scrambled to gather them up, the older sister felt a quick spasm of contriteness. Nancy had been talking as though all the trouble was over! Perhaps Granny's eyes had filled with tears and that was why she had spilled the hulls.

Harriet dropped her handfuls of hulls into the apron and leaned over to kiss Granny on the forehead. "Nancy hasn't forgotten about Uncle Matt," she said quietly. "It's just that we both are so happy about the mine's not getting dynamited."

Granny straightened her shoulders and smiled up at the girl bending above her. "That's all right, honey. Take one trouble at a time, and when one's over and behind, face the next one."

Grasping her apron with one hand, Granny then held out the pan of peas with the other. "Put these in the pot, Harriet," she said briskly. "And you, Nancy, mend that fire right away. I've got to get the bread on for dinner. There'll be a passel o' hungry folks here in a little while and no mistake."

But she interrupted her plans for dinner to glance out at her patient.

"He's got his eyes shut," she reported, "but I don't believe he's asleep for his breath comes too short and quick. We must be careful," she added in a low voice, "what we say in earshot o' him. No tellin' how long he'll stay here with us, and we'll just be obliged to get used to him. We must treat him mannerly, too. It's the only way to do."

"Yes, Granny," agreed Harriet, but she was thinking how hard it would be for everybody to be mannerly to Mr. Jones. This would be like being polite to a shoe that hurt your corns when you walked in it.

Uncle Matt and the boys entertained the family throughout dinner with an enthusiastic report of the work on the Orchard Hill homeplace.

"As soon as we get in the windows, we can move in," Dick declared. "Oh, there's a lot more to be done, little things inside and out, but they can be done mostly after we move and are settled down. We'll have to build new steps soon, clean up around the cabin, and put up a fence."

"I can nail on the palings, I guess," said John. "See, I'm growing a muscle," and he rolled up a shirt sleeve.

"So am I," declared Joan, displaying one to match her twin's.

"I can hammer!" announced Billy Boy with a prideful air. "I did it this morning. I drove a nail," he boasted, then paused to look about the table.

"What you all laugh for?" he demanded.

Bob slapped him on the back. "We're proud of you, Billy Boy! You can work and no mistake!"

"Well, I'm glad to hear that." And Uncle Matt looked across at him. "Maybe now I can get you to help me drive to town this afternoon."

Billy Boy squealed with delight.

"Humph!" remarked Granny. "You'll have that young 'un spoiled plumb to death until his folks won't own him when they see him again."

"When are they coming?" Aunt Lissie looked up at Harriet.

"Soon, I hope, real soon," was the reply. "There's no time set. They'll come when we have the cabin ready for them."

"That won't be long. You write and tell 'em to come right on, if they want to." This from Uncle Matt. "We'll be ready in a few days, anyway."

It was a cheerful scene in the kitchen. But it was one that for all its pleasant air seemed a little forced, as though it had stepped out of a play with rather self-conscious actors speaking brightly and a bit too loudly to keep up their courage.

Out in the dogtrot, propped up on his pallet bed with his ever-present coat behind his head, Mr. Jones ate his generous dinner in solitude. Several times during the meal Granny or Aunt Lissie went out to inquire about his wants or replenish his plate for him.

"We must be mannerly," Granny kept repeating as she set an example which maintained her own interpretation of good conduct.

In the afternoon after the boys had departed for the cabin, some callers came, as if by happenstance, to see Mr.

Jones. Granny received them all cordially. Catching up on her knitting, she sat down in the dogtrot with them. Aunt Lissie was there, too, with some mending. Near her, Harriet and Nancy sorted out the week's stockings.

Last among the callers were Buck Coomer and his father.

"Heard you got hurt and thought I'd drop by to see how you are coming along," Mr. Coomer said with an embarrassed air as he sat down in the chair Granny pushed forward for him. It had been many a year since he had come to this cabin.

Mr. Jones did not reply.

Mr. Coomer cleared his throat and began again. "Too bad about your accident." Beside him, Buck frowned at the injured man.

Still, Mr. Jones said nothing.

Again Mr. Coomer cleared his throat. "Too bad you started for the mine after sundown. It's hard to go a certain direction in these mountains after sunset," he went on. Then, suddenly leaning forward, he looked into Mr. Jones' face with eyes that seemed to drill through him.

"I guess you know what I've come for," he said angrily.

Mr. Jones' face flushed red under its pallor, and his face muscles twitched.

"No, I don't," he retorted and turned his face to the wall.

Mr. Coomer rose from his chair then and took a step toward the cot. Breathlessly, Harriet watched him. He looked exactly as though he were going to take hold of Mr. Jones and shake him soundly! Buck, too, was now standing up, his hands clenched.

Mr. Coomer took a step toward the cot.

"Well," exclaimed Granny cheerily, "I guess that's about as much visitin' as our invalid can stand at one stretch. There comes Matt, Mr. Coomer. How about our steppin' out a way to greet him?"

With a last angry glance at the back of Mr. Jones' head, Mr. Coomer walked from the dogtrot with Granny. And Buck slipped to Harriet's side, holding out a note.

"It's from Mary Ann," he explained. "About school."

"Thank you, Buck," Harriet smiled.

Buck moved one bare foot up and down a crack of the dogtrot floor. "I'm coming to school Monday," he stated, glancing up shyly.

"Oh, Buck! I'm glad. I have lots of new plans, and we need another ball player, too. Can you pitch?"

Buck blushed. "Guess so. Used to could, anyhow."

"That's fine! Be sure to come early, won't you? We always have one game before school takes up in the morning."

Buck nodded and then followed his father through the gate, arriving at his side just as Uncle Matt came driving up with Billy Boy.

"Howdy!" Uncle Matt cried cordially. "Left the windows at the cabin, folks. Every one's as sound as a dollar. I reckon the boys'll get them in come Monday, anyway."

"We've been to town," Billy Boy shouted.

Mr. Coomer nodded and then walked alongside of the wagon as it came up to the cabin. "Can you and me have a talk, Matt?" he asked earnestly, but in so friendly a voice that Harriet felt no dismay.

Uncle Matt glanced keenly down at his visitor and then jumped from the wagon and replied, "How about over there on that log?"

Granny held out her arms for Billy Boy, and Buck climbed into the wagon to drive the horses around to the barn.

"What do you suppose they're talking about, Harriet?" Nancy asked, nodding toward the two men.

"Whatever it is, Uncle Matt's mighty interested," replied Harriet. "Maybe he knows something that will help Uncle Matt out of his trouble."

"Don't you girls go gettin' your hopes up that-a-way," commented Granny, at their elbow. "It's a downright, sure-enough miracle to have the two of 'em sittin' there in peace, talkin' like neighbors."

"But, Granny—" Harriet began and then stopped and walked toward the porch. Inside the cabin, she hurriedly opened Mary Ann's note:

Dear Harriet:

    Pappy just told Buck and Buck told me that Pappy's not got any more use for that Mr. Jones. I'm glad of it, and I think Pappy's going over to your place to tell him a thing or two, and it's about something else besides the dynamiting. I don't know just what it is, but that Jones will soon have worse than a sprained ankle if some folks get ahold of him. There's talk around.

Goodbye till Monday.

Mary Ann

Harriet looked up to encounter Nancy's earnest gaze. "It's about our guest," she explained, folding up the note. "And something, Mary Ann doesn't know what, that is making folks awfully mad at him. Not just the dynamiting plan, I mean. I wonder—"

"Are you going to write Mother and Father that they can come any time now?" Nancy asked eagerly.

Harriet nodded. "Yes, and you'll be on hand for *that* excitement, Nancy."

When Mr. Coomer and Buck had left, Uncle Matt walked slowly into the kitchen and motioned Granny and Aunt Lissie to come out to the barn.

"Yes, you and Nancy can come, too, if you've a mind," he said in response to Harriet's pleading look.

Inside the barn, Uncle Matt turned to them with a puzzled little frown. "It's Jones," he explained, "and more of his tricks. Seems he's been gettin' money from the men, promisin' 'em they'll more than get it back from their bigger pay. He had it all worked out, it seems. Like a drawing! First, he got them to pay for his working things out, and they was to dynamite the mine. Then he was going to walk in and tell the mine owners what for. Then the pay envelopes was goin' to be bigger, right away and just like that. And now the men don't believe it at all. They're glad they didn't do the dynamitin', for a fact, Granny. And they want their money back. That's what Coomer come here to see Jones for, and Jones wouldn't say a word, just flopped over onto his coat. But Coomer's coming back, and he asked me was I goin' to keep a watch on him so that he won't get away with that money. Coomer thinks he has it on him. In his coat, maybe."

Harriet spoke up quickly. "Oh, no, Uncle Matt. Dick looked in his coat. There wasn't anything in the pockets at all."

"What's that? Dick searched his coat? Why?"

"Well," replied Harriet, reluctantly, "you know how he and Bob have been looking for a clue. They've had the idea that Mr. Jones used that hook to get the bag, and Dick was hunting for the money in his coat."

Slowly Uncle Matt shook his head. "I wish 'twas as simple as that, child. I only wish it was. Where that mail money's gone maybe never will be clear. And—"

"—and right now Coomer needn't be worrying about that guest of ours," said Granny decidedly. "He's a sick man, and he won't be starting off yet while. I've been nurse to more than one as banged up as he is, and I know a thing or two about 'em. Just you all go on treating him mannerly, and the men can get their money from him in due course. What have they decided about going back to work, Matt?"

Uncle Matt smiled. "They're going back, all right. And I said to Coomer if they think they should have more pay, why don't they get three or four of 'em to have a good talk with the foreman? And Coomer, he said we should have a committee, and he said Granny Murray had ought to be on it."

For answer, Granny hurried toward the barn door. "That's real nice, I'm sure," she called over her shoulder. "But the kitchen's my place, I'm thinkin', and I'm on my way there now!"

Chapter 15
Another Runaway

There was a different spirit in the school the following Monday, which manifested itself as soon as Harriet walked through the door. She was always sensitive to subtle changes in the attitude of those about her and was now aware at once that she was surrounded by a happier atmosphere.

For one thing, she found herself being regarded with admiration and even awe by all the children. For another, gifts of fruit—apples, grapes, and peaches—were heaped upon her table-desk.

"I can't imagine why they are doing this!" she exclaimed to Mary Ann Coomer, who lingered near. "Are these gifts peace offerings for mischief-making?"

"No, I reckon not," said Mary Ann, "but you might call 'em goodwill offerings, I guess, or thank offerings, maybe, sort o' like the kind the people gave back in Bible times."

But Harriet was still perplexed. "I can't riddle it out at all, as Granny Murray would say," she said, trying to read the mystery behind Mary Ann's expression, and failing utterly to do so.

Mary Ann's lips curved into a grin, and then her face sobered a little.

"It was your Granny that saved Middle Mine from being dynamited, and you helped her. Everybody's glad the dynamiting didn't happen."

"Oh," said Harriet, "I didn't do a thing. The men have all the women to thank for saving them from that foolishness. But I'm glad Granny's plan worked. I don't mind saying to you though, Mary Ann, that I was all atremble with pure fright for a little while. It was Granny's speech that saved me from heart failure. Wasn't she just splendid!"

"Yes," agreed Mary Ann, "I'll never forget her standing there and talking to all that crowd in front of her. She wasn't a bit afraid, or if she was she didn't show it. I heard my pappy and mammy talking about it afterwards, and Pappy laughed and said nobody could make a better speech than that, not even the Circuit Rider!"

"I'll have to tell Granny that. Just the other day she was saying she lacked 'the gift of gab' possessed by some people. She was talking about that Jones and the way he can get folks to do things in spite of their own reason. But that's over now."

"How long is he going to stay at your house?" asked Mary Ann. "It does seem sort o' funny his harboring under the very roof of the folks he plotted against. Everyone knows he started the story that your Uncle Matt stole the mail money."

"He did?" exclaimed Harriet. "I hadn't heard that!" Then in a moment, she continued, "But we couldn't refuse him shelter, not now that he is crippled, could we?"

"I guess not," Mary Ann admitted rather reluctantly. "How long will he be there?"

"Another week—maybe longer. He was whittling on a crutch this morning," said Harriet, "but I don't suppose he can use it for a good while. Granny dresses his foot twice every day."

Buck poked his head in at the open door. "Come on and play ball!" he shouted, then vanished.

Harriet looked at the watch. "It's nearly time to take up school, but I guess an extra quarter of an hour won't hurt. It's a celebration, really, of Buck's coming to school today."

"He took a notion," Mary Ann said, by way of explanation for Buck's sudden conversion to education. Harriet nodded. Everyone was glad to have Buck come. He was a good ball player and no mistake.

But Buck's return meant far more than that, Harriet thought. It was one more step in wiping out the Murray-Coomer feud. How happy her father and mother would be to come back and find Thunderhead Mountain a place of friendliness!

For a moment, she thought happily of the little cabin among the apple trees. Then quickly elation gave way to depression. Uncle Matt must still face a court trial. The miners' money had not been discovered. The robber had not been found.

All through that day at school, these thoughts recurred. When going home that afternoon, she met Squire Caudil; she asked anxiously, "They can't prove that Uncle Matt took that money. And you know he didn't."

"Yes, I do know he didn't," Squire Caudil answered gravely. "But I'm not the jury, and I'm not the judge. They're the ones who'll decide. That's all I can say. What I hope is another matter."

At home, Harriet found a letter from her father. "Oh, Granny," she cried when she had read the first paragraph—and there was a catch in her voice. "They can't come yet. The doctor says Mother should get more strength back before they try the trip. She has had a setback." And her lips quivered.

"Now, now, child, don't you take it so to heart. Their not comin' right now'll give you all that much more time to do some of the things you're countin' on. And when they do get here, they'll be right at home. Besides—" But Granny did not complete her sentence. And Harriet, hurrying out to tell the others of the Murray Six, did not ask what she had in mind. For she knew. "Besides, maybe things will work out for Matt by that time," Granny had meant to say. Poor Granny!

As the days passed, it became more and more evident that even Mr. Jones' strongest supporters had turned against him. The men returned to work in the mine, appointing a committee as Uncle Matt had suggested. And the foreman had been quite frank in giving them a picture of the actual condition of the mine. He had even shown them the books—and from the figures the men had been convinced of the owners' fairness.

Uncle Matt continued his work as watchman with no ugly insinuations being cast upon his innocence. If it had not been for the court trial, Granny and her family would have been entirely happy in their anticipation of the coming arrival of the parents of the Murray Six.

Every now and then, some of Mr. Jones' former admirers appeared and tried to get from him information as to the whereabouts of the money they had paid him. But to every question, Mr. Jones replied only with a sulky silence. When some of the men suggested more strenuous measures to extract the desired answers, Granny took a firm hand.

"That you will not do," she declared. "You've got to treat invalids mannerly—'specially guests."

As the day for Uncle Matt's trial came ever closer, however, it seemed to Harriet that Granny's insistence upon mannerliness sounded half-hearted. Indeed, all the family was now feeling the strain. Nerves got jumpy; patience grew thin. To make matters worse, the Murray Six had no definite date ahead for their parents' arrival. If only they could have known when Mother and Father would be there, Harriet felt sure they would be helped tremendously. But an increasing sense of dread was with them all.

Only Billy Boy and John and Joan went their way with any degree of lightheartedness.

The Mail Wagon Mystery

One afternoon while Harriet was helping get supper in the kitchen, Joan and John came slipping through the door and took Mr. Jones' coat to use in a game they were playing. They ran outside.

A few minutes later, Mr. Jones gave a loud groan that resembled a roar. Granny left the corner cupboard where she had been sorting the dishes, crossed to the open door, and very kindly said, "Are you in misery, Mr. Jones? What seems to ail you?"

Another groan was the only reply. Granny hurried to his side. Mr. Jones was now holding his head in his hands and shaking as if he had the ague.

"He's had a relapse, I reckon," cried Granny, laying a firm hand on the quaking shoulder. "Better lie back on your bed, Mr. Jones."

"My coat—my coat!" Mr. Jones moaned, shaking off her hand.

"What you need is a blanket," said Granny, "and a hot rock at your feet. I'll tend to you in no time."

For answer, Mr. Jones struggled to his feet, using his crutch to support himself.

"Where is my coat, my coat?" he demanded. "It was here, and now it is gone!"

"Never mind, never mind," Granny replied, soothingly. "It's around somewhere, I reckon. I'll get you a bed blanket, then I'll look for it." And she vanished in the direction of the big bedroom.

Mr. Jones hobbled to the kitchen door. "Where's my coat?" he demanded fiercely of Harriet, who jumped in startled surprise at his words.

"Your coat, Mr. Jones? I don't know anything about it. Maybe somebody hung it up. I'll look for it as soon as I get the bread on."

Mr. Jones hobbled back to his pallet. And Harriet, washing her hands quickly, paused at the kitchen door to consider the problem.

At that minute Billy Boy ran pell-mell through the yard, the twins after him. He was hugging a bundle closely.

Harriet took one glance at it, saw, and understood. It was Mr. Jones' old coat, rolled into a rectangular bundle and tied with a knot in the sleeves. It was what the twins had been talking about when they came through the kitchen.

"Come here, Billy Boy," she said. "That's Mr. Jones' coat. You must give it back to him. No, wait. You twins ought to do that."

"All right," they both said, and off they went, the coat dangling between them.

"Here, Mr. Jones, here's your coat," they shouted. Then they dashed away leaving the coat on a chair near the invalid, as if fearful to approach within reaching distance of the dark man who sat hunched up on his pallet bed, trying to resist Granny's gentle yet firm ministrations.

"Here, let me fold this blanket around you, and you drink this hot tea," Granny said. "It'll chase the chill right out o' your bones."

Mr. Jones paid no attention to her. Reaching out, he pulled the coat over to his pallet and bundled it under his head.

Billy Boy ran pell-mell through the yard.

"Leave me in peace," he muttered ungratefully. And Granny, at the end of all patience, cried, "I think you must be possessed. I never saw such a cross-grained man."

She was stamping angrily as she returned to the kitchen. "The next time he groans, I vow I'll be in no hurry to hasten to him. Be good to your enemies. That's what the Good Book says, but I leave it all to the angels above if I've not done more than my duty. Harriet, the bread's burnin'—don't you smell it? Harriet! Where are you?"

But Harriet was gone. And Granny, still in the grip of hot indignation, crossed to the stove and herself attended to the bread. Had she gone to the back door, she would have seen her oldest granddaughter gazing in amazement at a ten-dollar bill.

After the scramble to return the coat, Harriet had noticed something lying on the kitchen floor. When stooping to pick it up, she had seen that it was a ten-dollar bill; her hands had trembled and her breath had come fast at the thought that came rushing to her mind. This money must have dropped from the coat while the children were playing. None of the family had that much! What if Dick had been right all along, and Mr. Jones was the thief, after all?

Almost blindly, she had hurried outside to be alone. And her hands trembled as she carefully examined the bill. Yes, it was real. Then her forehead wrinkled as she tried to recall just what Dick had done that night when he examined the pockets of Mr. Jones' coat. Had he really looked in every one? He had been in such a hurry, surely he might easily have overlooked one on the inside.

Yes, that was what must have happened. And because the money was still there, Mr. Jones had kept his coat under his head, for a pillow. Of course! He was the one who had taken the mail money. All they needed to do now was to get the coat and—she was just about to rush inside and tell Granny the good news when another thought held her back.

Was she sure this was the mine money? Mr. Coomer and the others had been coming to see about what they had paid over to Mr. Jones. They had never said just how much they had given him, but it must have been more than ten dollars. In which case, this bill could just as well be the men's, and not the mine money at all.

From inside the kitchen came the sound of Granny's movements as she went on with the supper preparations. Poor Granny! It would be cruel even to suggest to her this possibility of clearing Uncle Matt when it might so easily prove only a false hope.

"Harriet! Nan—cee! Harriet!"

It was the twins, shouting of some discovery just made out by the barn. Quickly Harriet thrust the bill into her apron pocket, the crisp bill that mocked her with its subtle hint of hope.

"Harriet!" Now it was Granny calling.

"Yes, Granny!" Harriet replied. "I'm coming!"

But before she returned to the kitchen, she paused to remove the bill from her apron pocket, fold it, and thrust it hastily down into the top of her shoe.

By the time she was once more at Granny's side, she had made up her mind what to do. She would say nothing to anyone until she had managed to get hold of Mr. Jones' coat again and examine it minutely. If she told anyone, something might be said that would arouse Mr. Jones' suspicions. Then there was no telling what he would do with the money—hide it somewhere perhaps, for he was hobbling about fairly well now. That is, he might hide it if there were any there to hide. Again and again, Harriet's thoughts returned to the realization that the ten dollars in the top of her shoe might be all there was…

Granny was lighting a pine stick on the hearth. "Even in midsummer," she said, "seems like there's a chill comes creeping along with the shadows. 'Tis lonesome unless you have a light kindled on the hearth then. It's pret-nigh time for supper. Go out into the porch, Harriet, and whoop everybody up."

Throughout that meal Harriet strove to present a casual manner, to betray no hint of the agitation that stirred the recesses of her mind. It was hard to keep her eyes from Mr. Jones' face, at the end of the table, for he was now able to come there with the aid of his crutch. Mealtime was always difficult, with him among them. Uncle Matt had ideas of duty to which he sternly bound himself with relentless chains. But neither manners nor morals compelled him to carry on a conversation with this person whom ironical chance had made his enemy-guest.

Aunt Lissie had become so nervous she could scarcely hold a spoonful of food without spilling it four different ways. And tonight even Granny seemed depressed or perhaps, Harriet thought, she was outraged by her failure to administer to her patient. At any rate, she paid attention to her plate and very little else.

No one made any comment when Harriet slipped away from her place at the table and disappeared into the darkness without. Nor did anyone question her when after a prolonged absence, she returned. Bob and Dick were talking in low tones on their side of the table, and Nancy was shamelessly eavesdropping. Only Billy Boy greeted her.

"More molasses, Harriet, please," he said.

Harriet sat down at her place at the table and glanced at Mr. Jones. He had eaten very little, seeming to be feasting mainly on his thoughts. Their flavor was not altogether savory, judging from his dour expression. Shortly after Harriet reappeared, he got up and hobbled away. In silence, the family listened as he thumped about in the dogtrot. Then the thud of his crutch stick sounded no more.

"Bad man's gone," observed Billy Boy. "Please, may I have more molasses?"

Harriet took his plate and tilted the old blue pitcher to pour a little trickle of brown sweetness on a piece of cornbread. Billy Boy's bread and molasses rarely gave out together, a circumstance due, Harriet suspected, to her small brother's clever management.

At length, Aunt Lissie rose and said, "I better shut up the chickens. Some varmint got into the barn roost last night, and this morning a pullet was gone."

Harriet was washing Billy Boy's face, the twins were getting ready for another game, Dick and Bob were considering what to do next, and Nancy was starting to help Granny with the supper dishes when Aunt Lissie rushed back. "Did you boys turn Dock into the pasture?" she asked breathlessly.

"No!" cried the boys together.

"He's not in the little lot," Aunt Lissie said, "and he's not about the barn. He must have broken out."

Uncle Matt and the boys jumped up from the table and dashed outside. When they came back, Uncle Matt was shaking with anger, but Dick and Bob announced the news:

"Dock—and Mr. Jones—both gone!"

"The varmint," muttered Uncle Matt, "and with the men's money, too."

Harriet pushed past him, into the darkness. When she returned, over her arm was Mr. Jones' old coat.

Chapter 16
Home on Orchard Hill

A chorus of exclamations greeted the sight.

"I played a trick on him," Harriet began quickly, "and it may all be to no purpose, so don't build up your expectations. It's just an idea I had, and it may not come to a thing."

Another chorus fell upon her ears.

"But why!"

"When—"

"What made you do it—swipe that old coat?" this from Dick.

For answer, Harriet stepped closer to the kerosene lamp on the kitchen table, the coat grasped firmly in her hands. The others pressed about her, anxiously following every move.

Rip—rip—and the lining admitted Harriet's eager right hand. "Yes, I do feel something," she said, feeling carefully about. Then, "Look!" and she drew out a handful of loose greenbacks and laid them on the table.

With startled exclamations, the rest of the family bent over the money. Wonderingly Uncle Matt picked it up and counted it. "Twenty-five dollars," he said. "It's the money the men paid him for the strike, I reckon."

"There is more here too, I think," Harriet went on, bending over the coat. "I feel it. The whole inside is lined with something tacked here and there."

Her quick fingers broke threads with a series of snaps that sounded loud in the intense silence which now fell upon the kitchen.

"There!" Harriet drew forth her hand once more to show them a ten-dollar bill.

It was too much. Dropping the money, Harriet sank down in a chair and gave a half-hysterical giggle. "Why, I must be dreaming," she said weakly.

"It's the money—the miners' money all right," muttered Uncle Matt, smoothing out the green bills on the table.

Ever since Harriet had produced the first handfuls of bills, Granny had seemed in a daze. Now, however, she sprang into action. "Give me that coat!" she cried. "I'm thinking the mine money's there with the rest of it."

Rip—snip—rip! It was only a matter of moments before Granny triumphantly added a goodly number of bills to those already on the table. With exulting count, Dick and Bob declaimed the total. Granny was right. Without doubt,

The Mail Wagon Mystery Page 141

Granny triumphantly added a goodly number of bills.

it was not only the mine money but what the miners had paid to Mr. Jones.

Thick and fast came the family's questions then. How had Harriet happened to think of looking there for the money? How had she managed to get hold of Mr. Jones' old coat? Had she known he was planning to go off? Why hadn't he missed his coat?

"Heaps o' money," exclaimed Billy Boy during a slight pause in the barrage of questioning.

Harriet smiled at her small brother and, bending over, took from the top of her shoe another ten-dollar bill.

"The clue to the mystery," she told them with a little flourish.

Interruptions started again, but Harriet held up her hand. "I'll tell you everything just as it happened if you'll let me begin at the beginning," she said.

"Go on, honey. That's right. Don't a one of you all interrupt her now till she gets through—not a one!" cried Granny in a severe tone, her black eyes snapping about the circle of faces from Uncle Matt to Billy Boy. Then she turned to Harriet. "Wag on with your tale, child." And she raised her walking stick to give it a thump upon the floor. "I'll keep 'em in line."

The circle around the table stood mute, and Harriet began. "It won't take long," she said, "but before I begin on what happened, I want to say I'm sorry I ever laughed at Dick and Bob and their clues, because they were right all along. Mr. Jones did take the mine money just the way they figured out."

In pleased embarrassment at being thus included in the glory of the moment, her brother and cousin grinned at her. But before Granny's intent eyes, they remained silent, waiting for Harriet's revelations.

"When Dick looked through the pockets of the coat that night, nobody would even have thought any money was in it," Harriet continued. "In fact, if it hadn't been for the twins, we never would have known. I guess you've all seen John and Joan slipping up on Mr. Jones when he was asleep and trying to touch his shadow or—"

"Or his foot," cried John.

"And his hair sometimes," added Joan.

Granny frowned fiercely in their direction and, reaching out her stick, prodded them into silence.

"Well," went on Harriet, "just before supper they had a new idea. They managed to get hold of his coat that he had been using for a pillow and—"

"But his head had slipped off, Harriet," explained John.

Harriet nodded. "Yes, his head had slipped off, and you snatched up the coat and ran off with it."

"Then Billy Boy grabbed it, and we didn't want him to have it," Joan put in.

"And that is how it got torn so that a ten-dollar bill dropped out onto the kitchen floor. I was so busy with supper, I didn't notice what they were scuffling over, to tell you the truth. The twins kept saying it was a bundle. So when they ran outdoors with it, I didn't think anything about it, one way or another. Then when Granny was out with Mr. Jones, I found the bill. And what with his shouting around about his coat being gone, I realized that was what the children had and this money must have dropped out of it.

"You know how he wouldn't let the coat out of his sight? We'd wondered why, so right away I thought this money must have been in a secret hiding place in it all along."

"The ill-turned wretch!" cried Granny.

Billy Boy bent a reproving eye upon his grandmother. "Mustn't interrupt, Granny!" he said.

Everyone laughed at that, then all once more turned toward Harriet.

"Well," went on Harriet, "the idea of its having been inside the lining popped into my head. I was just going to tell Granny about it when I remembered how worried she'd been about Uncle Matt and how disappointed she'd be if the ten dollars I'd found was all there was. And it might have been, you know. So I stuck the bill into my shoe and made up my mind to get that coat some way and find out.

"While we were eating supper, and Mr. Jones was acting even more queer than usual, all of a sudden I noticed he didn't have his coat on. And I thought then and there I'd better go out and look. I couldn't find it at first—it was all rolled up and under the bottom of the pallet. I guess he didn't want to wear it into supper for fear Granny would want to mend the tear, and he didn't want her poking into it. Anyway, by that time I was afraid he'd be coming out, so I grabbed up that old coat of Uncle Matt's that's always hanging outside and rolled it up the same way he did his when he used it as a pillow. Then I put it under the pallet and took his coat out back. I didn't have any idea he'd be running off the way he did. I just thought he'd lie down without making a light, as he always has, you know, and wouldn't miss his own coat until I'd had time to search it. But you know all the rest!" she cried, ending abruptly.

It was Dick who spoke first. "I'd like to see that fellow," he said, "when he takes time to look at Uncle Matt's coat!"

"So would I!" Bob shouted. "And I'll bet he sets the air afire for a mile around with the words he'll have to say."

Nancy shivered. "I'm glad he's gone. Living with him under our roof was dreadful. Why anything, *anything* could have happened."

Granny roused herself from her silent reflections. "The Lord looks after us," she said, and to Billy Boy and the twins, "Come along now, all you young 'uns. It's time to turn in."

When they were gone, Harriet said, "I'm sorry about your coat, Uncle Matt. I just had to use it."

"You say something to me?" he asked, lifting his head from long contemplation of the treasure spread out upon the table. His eyes blinked in the lamplight. "Did you speak to me, some of you?"

"Never mind," Harriet said, and she made a motion to the rest. Uncle Matt must be left without interruption for a little while to think about the good fortune that had come to him.

Harriet followed a winding trail through the apple orchard, writing materials tucked under her arm. She was seeking her favorite tree—a gnarled old giant whose canopy of twisted and interlaced branches bent over like a giant umbrella, a sun-proof tent which made an ideal retreat for her rare escapes from the activity at the cabin.

Orchard Hill was a lovely place this Saturday morning in early October. The air was redolent with the fragrance of ripe and mellow fruit. The browning grass had the scent of hay. Along the creek in the valley, sycamores were yellowing, and the spur of the mountain beyond spread out bright banners of sassafras gold and the royal scarlet of sumac. It was a lovely time, Harriet thought, for a welcome home, as Granny Murray called the coming of Father and Mother.

Spreading a sheet of paper on her knee, she began her letter to them. After the greeting she paused. Her last letter before their homecoming! Yes, and it must be a nice letter—a good letter, full of happy description. She would make a word picture for them of the house on Orchard Hill. She would tell how it had been finished and furnished, till at last it was ready to be a real home for them. They would like to hear how the neighbors and kin had lent kind hands to the labor so that the homecoming would be hastened. She would tell how this and that one had brought gifts for the house, things of prided possession. "Nothing's too good for our own folks that are coming back to us," Mary Ann's mother had said when she brought over this very morning a coverlet bright as a flower bed, in the Rainbow Ring pattern, pieced years ago. Some of the patches in it were even cut from dress scraps Harriet's mother had given Mary Ann's mother one day, long ago.

It made an ideal retreat for her rare escapes from the cabin.

Squire Caudil had given a rocking chair which had belonged to his mother, "I'm getting a little too hefty to risk myself in it," he had said. "Just about the right size for a small woman person, 'bout like your mammy, I guess."

Mother would appreciate that, though it would be a great wonder if she didn't get a bit hefty herself if she ate one half of the good things that Granny and Aunt Lissie were planning to feed her—chicken and dewberry jelly, the salt rising rolls and fresh milk, and dozens of other things.

The letter grew from one page to ten. The morning sun crept over the hill and seemed to halt for a while above Harriet's apple tree, poking a long yellow finger down through the rustling branches, as if he were curious to read for himself the pages that slipped from her knee.

She had better close, thought Harriet, or she would not be able to get it all folded properly into an envelope.

Yes, she must stop—she couldn't tell *everything* in a letter. Then, too, so much had happened this past week that she hadn't even mentioned—all this she had left out on purpose. Later on, Father and Mother would hear all about the trouble on Thunderhead. How wonderful that it was over before Father and Mother came home!

Perhaps she could go on teaching school here, saving her money to educate herself better. She could attend the spring and summer terms at the state university. Then she could help the other children later when they outgrew the little mountain school. Perhaps the Murrays could all make a real home here on Thunderhead Mountain among their own people. Father's services were needed too, as a minister and friend. Harriet realized that he would feel the change in the people now. He would surely be welcomed and wanted, now that all the trouble was over.

For it was over. Mr. Jones had been caught by officers who had been looking for him for a long time. Squire Caudil had brought along the Nashville newspaper that described his capture. It seemed that Jones was only one of several names under which he had lived for the past ten years. And wherever he had gone, during all those years, trouble had followed.

He would always seem like an ogre to the folk on Thunderhead Mountain, Harriet thought. Legends would grow up about him no doubt, in the years to come, and when the twins and Billy Boy were grown up they would remember with mild shudders their dark guest.

"Harriet. O—oh, Harriet!" It was Nancy.

"Coming!" Harriet called and got to her feet.

"Harriet—quick!"

Was Nancy in trouble? Harriet ran up the path.

"What—what—is it?" she managed to say as she opened the gate and left it swinging.

"I can't find the flavoring," Nancy called. "I'm making an apple pie."

Harriet laughed with relief. "There isn't any, I guess," she said, coming into the kitchen and smiling at her earnest sister-cook. Then she brushed off a smudge of flour from one flushed cheek and kissed Nancy on the nose.

"That's a 'thank you' for my piece when it's done. And never mind the flavoring. When folks are hungry, plain apple pie is a real treat!"

More Books from The Good and the Beautiful Library!

His Indian Brother
by Hazel Wilson

Redwood Pioneer
by Betty Stirling

Slave Boy in Judea
by Josephine Sanger Lau

Zeke and the Fisher-Cat
by Virginia Frances Voight

goodandbeautiful.com